A King Production presents…

A Titillating Tale

A Novelette

Joy Deja King

This novelette is a work of fiction. Any references to real people, events, establishments, or locales are intended only to give the fiction a sense of reality and authenticity. Other names, characters, and incidents occurring in the work are either the product of the author's imagination or are used fictitiously, as those fictionalized events and incidents that involve real persons. Any character that happens to share the name of a person who is an acquaintance of the author, past or present, is purely coincidental and is in no way intended to be an actual account involving that person.

ISBN 13: 978-1-958834-85-5
ISBN 10: 1-958834-85-8
Cover concept by Joy Deja King
Library of Congress Cataloging-in-Publication Data;
A King Production
Mastermind 2...Serenity's Revenge by Joy Deja King
Typesetting: www.anitaart79.wixsite.com/bookdesign

For complete Library of Congress Copyright info visit; www.joydejaking.com
Twitter @joydejaking

A King Production
P.O. Box 912, Collierville, TN 38027
A King Production and the above portrayal log are trademarks of A King Production LLC

Copyright © 2025 by A King Production LLC. All rights reserved. No part of this book may be reproduced in any form without the permission from the publisher, except by reviewer who may quote brief passage to be printed in a newspaper or magazine.

This Novelette is Dedicated To My:

Family, Readers and Supporters.
I LOVE you guys so much. Please believe that!!

~ Joy Deja King ~

A special THANK YOU to my amazing sister Robin, for being the inspiration for this titillating tale.

~ Joy Deja King ~

"It Was All My Design
'Cause I'm A Mastermind ..."

A KING PRODUCTION

Mastermind 2...
Serenity's Revenge

A Novelette

JOY DEJA KING

Chapter One

The Mask Of Loyalty

Lila Richardson sat behind the glass desk, the morning sun casting a warm glow through the floor-to-ceiling windows of her corner office. She was a picture of poise and power. The Atlanta City skyline sprawled behind her, a reflection of the empire she now controlled. CR Enterprises had once been synonymous with Cartier Richardson's dominance in the advertising industry, but now it bore her touch—a blend of elegance and precision.

Dressed in a tailored to perfection black suit, the silk blouse beneath it adding a hint of softness to her otherwise sharp image, and crimson stilettos. A Montblanc pen rolled idly between her fingers as she reviewed the Langston contract on her desk. She paused, glancing at the gold nameplate that still read *Cartier Richardson*. It was deliberate. Keeping Cartier's name visible was a calculated move, a way to maintain appearances while she solidified her reign.

To the outside world, she was the victim of her husband's cruelty, a phoenix rising from the ashes of betrayal. Only Lila knew the truth: Cartier's downfall had been entirely her design. She had worked too hard, played too many games, and pulled too many strings to falter now. Every detail of her ascension to power had been orchestrated flawlessly—the supposed attempt on her life, the carefully planted evidence, and Cartier's subsequent arrest.

The thought of Cartier—his arrogance, his betrayals, and the years of lies—sent a ripple of bitterness through her. He'd thought he could humiliate her with his endless parade of mistresses, thought he could discard her while she played the dutiful wife. But she'd shown him.

The plan had been risky, but it had worked.

Framing him for her attempted murder and the murder of Cynthia had ensured he'd never walk free again. Callie had been collateral damage, caught in the crossfire, but Lila had no regrets. In the end, Cartier was behind bars with one of his former mistresses, and CR Enterprises was hers.

Lila leaned back in her chair, her hand absentmindedly toying with the Montblanc pen Cartier had once used to sign his deals. Now it was hers, just like everything else he thought he controlled. But even as she basked in her triumph, a shadow of unease lingered. She couldn't shake the feeling that Serenity—smart, resourceful Serenity—saw through her. A knock at the door broke her reverie.

"Come in," she called, her voice calm and commanding.

Serenity stepped in, radiant in a cream blazer and matching trousers, her long braids falling elegantly over her shoulders. She was a vision of grace and professionalism. She held a notebook tucked under her arm; her smile polite but faintly guarded. Exuding the quiet confidence that had earned her a permanent place at Lila's side.

"Serenity," Lila said warmly, gesturing toward the sitting area near the windows. "Come, sit. We need to talk before the Langston meeting."

"Of course," Serenity nodded, as she approached taking a seat on the cream leather couch. Her smile never wavered as she folded her hands neatly in her lap. "What's on your mind?"

Lila sat across from her, crossing her legs with a practiced grace. Her tone softened, taking on the air of someone trying to repair a fragile bond. "I've been meaning to speak to you, Serenity. About... everything."

Serenity tilted her head slightly, feigning curiosity. "Everything?"

Lila's expression grew pained, her eyes lowering briefly before meeting Serenity's again. "What happened with Cartier. The... attempt on my life. It's still difficult to talk about, but I owe you an apology."

Serenity raised an eyebrow, leaning forward. "An apology?"

Lila nodded; her tone heavy with manufactured regret, her voice lowering. "I want to say sorry again for misleading you. For letting you believe, even for a moment, that I was dead. It wasn't fair to you. But I didn't have a choice, Serenity. You have to understand—I was desperate. I didn't know who I could trust."

Serenity's stomach churned at the blatant manipulation, but she forced herself to look sympathetic. "You were trying to survive," she said quietly. "I can't imagine what you went through, Lila. Knowing that Cartier... that he could...I truly understand your dilemma."

Lila's eyes glistened and she swallowed hard, leaning back as though the recollection pained her. "I trusted him, Serenity. I gave him everything. And for what? Years of cheating, lies, and humiliation. And then to think he would try to kill me..." She shook her head, her voice trembling just enough to sound sincere. She looked away, as if lost in the memory. "It broke me, Serenity. It really did."

Serenity's eyes narrowed ever so slightly, her pulse quickened, the lie hitting her like a slap. She knew the truth: Cartier had done no such thing. Lila had orchestrated everything, planting the evidence, spinning the narrative, framing him for attempted murder and killing Cynthia, to destroy him, claim his estate, and seize control of his empire. Yet here she was, playing the victim to perfection.

"You've been through hell, Lila," Serenity said, her voice steady despite the fire burning inside her. But she kept her voice steady, her expression calm. "I'm still trying to make sense of it all."

Lila smiled faintly, her gaze softening. "Me too. When Cartier was arrested... I know how much you cared for him, Serenity. It must have been so hard for you, turning him in."

Serenity tensed, but only for a moment. She nodded, her tone quiet and measured. "It wasn't easy. But he tried to kill you and murdered poor Cynthia. I had to do the right thing. I can't imagine how hard it must have been for you."

"It was," Lila said, her lips tightening. Then, as if shaking off the weight of the memory, she straightened and looked Serenity in the eye. "But I'm here now. And I'm stronger because of it. Thanks to you."

"Me?" Serenity appeared perplexed.

"Yes. You've been my rock," Lila said, her voice warm with gratitude. "You did the right thing, Serenity. You stood for justice. And because of you, CR Enterprises is thriving."

Serenity clenched her jaw subtly, keeping her outward calm. Lila was masterful in her manipulation, spinning a web of lies with an elegance that almost made Serenity admire her. Almost.

"I just wanted to do what was best for you and the company."

"And you did," Lila said firmly. "You did the

right thing, Serenity. And I promise, it won't go unrewarded. After we finalize the Langston deal, you'll be receiving a promotion and a well-deserved pay raise."

Serenity smiled, though she wanted to vomit. "Thank you, Lila. That means a lot to me."

Lila reached out, resting a hand on Serenity's arm. "I don't say it enough, but I couldn't have done this without you. I'm grateful every day that you're by my side."

Serenity's lips curved into a soft, placid smile. "I will always have your back." The words felt like acid on her tongue, but Lila didn't notice.

"We have a busy few weeks ahead of us. First the Langston meeting today and getting the contracts signed before the end of the month, also the upcoming corporate gala. Make sure you're ready for both."

"I will be." Serenity gave a polite smile.

As she rose to leave, Lila called after her, "Serenity?"

Serenity turned, her hand on the doorknob.

"I know you loved him," Lila said gently. "Cartier. That kind of love doesn't just go away. If you ever need to talk about it, I'm here for you."

Serenity's smile remained in place, but her

eyes darkened slightly. "Thank you, Lila. I'll keep that in mind."

As Serenity left the office, her calm demeanor didn't falter, but the moment the door closed behind her, her expression hardened. The polite smile fell away, replaced by a steely determination.

You're good, Lila, she thought. *You think you've won. But I know what you did. When the time is right, I'll make sure the world knows too. Your time is coming. You took Cartier down, and now it's your turn.*

Lila could enjoy her illusion of power for now, but Serenity was playing the long game. And this time, the queen would fall because the real mastermind was only just getting started.

Chapter Two

New Reign

Serenity's heels clicked against the polished floors of the hallway as she left Lila's office, her pace deliberate and steady. The soft murmur of employees at their desks and the faint hum of office chatter surrounded her, but Serenity heard none of it. She replayed Lila's carefully crafted lies and her audacious offer of sympathy.

"I know you loved him. Cartier."

The words burned in Serenity's chest. Love hadn't blinded her to Cartier's flaws—his arrogance, his secrets, the way he could charm and manipulate his way out of anything. But beneath all of that, there had been a man she believed in, a man she thought could change. A man she now realized had been betrayed by his own wife.

Lila conned us all, Serenity thought, her mind racing as she entered her own office. She shut the door behind her, leaning against it for a moment to gather herself. The sleek, modern space felt colder than usual, its minimalist design mirroring the calculated persona she had adopted to survive in Lila's world. Serenity walked to her desk and sank into the chair, pulling open the bottom drawer. From it, she retrieved a small leather-bound notebook.

The notebook was filled with notes, scribbled in her handwriting, detailing every piece of evidence she had uncovered about Lila's betrayal. She spent the last few months piecing it together: the forged documents, the anonymous tips to the authorities, the planted evidence that had led to Cartier's arrest. Serenity flipped to the most recent page, her pen hovering over the paper. She wrote two words at the top of the page: *Next Move.*

Her strategy needed to be flawless. Lila had stolen Cartier's empire based on lies and manipulation. Tearing it down would require patience. If she moved too quickly, Lila would crush her without hesitation. But if she played her cards right, Lila's carefully constructed world would crumble around her.

Months earlier, right after Cartier's arrest, Serenity was devastated. She had been the one to provide key information to the authorities, believing she was bringing a dangerous man to justice. But when she overheard Lila bragging to Bradley about her well executed scheme, Serenity realized she had been duped. Bringing Lila down would require more than just overhearing a conversation; solid, irrefutable evidence would be necessary. Serenity began sifting through key data and noticed the cracks in Lila's story.

It had started with a misplaced email—an overlooked message in Lila's inbox that referenced an offshore account linked to the planted data against Cartier and Callie. Then there were the security camera logs that had been altered to incriminate Cartier. Serenity was still trying to find evidence to link Lila and Bradley to Cynthia's murder and the "so called" poison used in the attempt on Lila's life.

However, there was one piece that had come in the form of a voice recording Serenity found in

Bradley's private files. Lila was having a conversation with one of her hired operatives, strategizing on how to set up the corporate espionage and racketeering allegations in order to make it seem like Cartier was responsible.

Hearing Lila's voice so calm, so calculated, had sent chills down Serenity's spine. That was the moment she knew the truth: Cartier had been framed, for those charges too and Lila was the real mastermind.

Serenity closed the notebook and slid it back into the drawer, locking it with a small key she kept on a chain around her neck. Her next step had to be subtle but decisive...a move that would destabilize Lila's hold without alerting her to the threat.

A soft knock at the door interrupted her thoughts.

"Come in," Serenity called, smoothing her expression into one of practiced cool.

Reese, her assistant, stepped inside, holding a folder. "The reports you asked for on the Langston deal," she said, placing it on the desk.

"Thank you, Reese," Serenity said, offering a brief smile.

Reese hesitated, shifting slightly. "If I may, Serenity... Are you okay? You've seemed... distracted lately."

"I'm fine. Just a lot on my plate."

Reese nodded, though her concern lingered. "If you need anything, let me know."

As Reese left, Serenity opened the folder, her eyes scanning the documents. Buried among the standard projections and updates was a section on an overseas subsidiary of CR Enterprises—a subsidiary Lila had quietly moved under her sole control shortly after Cartier's arrest.

Serenity's lips curved into a small, cold smile. *Gotcha.*

Later that day, Serenity joined the other executives in the conference room for the Langston deal presentation. The senior executives sat around the table, discussing terms and logistics waiting for Lila to arrive and command the room with her effortless confidence. But Serenity's focus wouldn't be on the deal. She wanted to study Lila's every move—the way she deflected tough questions; the way she leaned into her charm to win over skeptical board members.

Right on cue, the polished mahogany doors of CR Enterprises' executive boardroom swung open, revealing Lila Richardson's silhouette framed in the threshold. Her presence sent an electric current through the air, silencing the murmurs of the gathered executives. With measured steps that echoed against the marble floor, Lila strode to the head of the table, her designer heels a staccato rhythm of authority.

Lila's gaze swept across the room, meeting each pair of eyes with a blend of warmth and steel. She allowed the tension to build, savoring the palpable anticipation. When she finally spoke, her voice was a velvet-wrapped blade.

"Good afternoon, everyone. I trust you're all as eager as I am to usher in this new venture for CR Enterprises merging with Langston International."

A chorus of polite agreement rippled through the room. Lila noted the varying degrees of enthusiasm, cataloging potential allies and adversaries.

"As your new CEO, I stand before you not just as a leader, but as a steward of our shared vision," she continued, her words carefully chosen to evoke both authority and camaraderie. "CR Enterprises has long been synonymous with luxury and excellence. Now, it's time we redefine what that means in today's rapidly evolving market."

Lila paused, allowing her words to sink in. She could feel the weight of expectation pressing down on her shoulders, a familiar burden she'd learned to bear with grace. Behind her placid expression, she was calculating each word, each gesture.

"Our path forward demands innovation, adaptability, and above all, unity," she declared, her voice rising with passion she only partially felt. "We must be willing to take calculated risks, to push boundaries, and to challenge our own preconceptions of what this company can achieve."

As she spoke, Lila moved around the table, her proximity a subtle assertion of dominance. She placed a hand on the shoulder of Bradley Upton, her most vocal supporter, feeling him straighten under her touch.

"I know change can be daunting," Lila admitted, her tone softening. "But I assure you, every decision I make will be in service of our collective success. Your expertise, your dedication – these are the pillars upon which we'll build our future."

Internally, Lila smirked at the irony of her words. She'd climb over every person in this room if it meant achieving her goals. But for now, she needed their trust, their loyalty and most importantly closing the Langston deal.

"I open the floor to your thoughts, your concerns," she offered, returning to her place at the head of the table. "After all, this is not my company – it's ours. And together, we will propel CR Enterprises and Langston International into a new era of unprecedented success."

As the executives began to voice their opinions, Lila leaned back slightly, her posture relaxed but alert. She'd laid the groundwork, sown the seeds of her vision. Now, it was time to watch them take root, to nurture some and ruthlessly prune others. The game had begun, and Lila Richardson intended to emerge victorious, no matter the cost.

At one point, Lila glanced at Serenity, her smile warm and genuine on the surface. But Serenity saw the glimmer of calculation in her eyes. Lila knew how to manipulate everyone around her, including Serenity.

Not for much longer, Serenity thought.

As Lila's honeyed words washed over the room, Serenity's mind raced, each thought a dagger of resentment.

"Bravo, Lila," she mused silently. "You've certainly perfected your performance."

The memory of Lila's betrayal seared through her consciousness, igniting a fierce resolve. Serenity's gaze drifted to the chair once claimed by Cartier, now occupied by Lila—a stark reminder of her ultimate mission.

When the meeting ended, Lila pulled Serenity aside. "You were quiet in there," Lila said, her tone light but probing.

"I didn't want to overstep," Serenity replied sweetly. "You've got everything under control."

Lila smiled, but there was a hint of suspicion in her gaze. "You've been so dependable, Serenity. I hope you know how much I appreciate you."

Serenity's face remained composed as she replied, "I do. Like I told you earlier today. I will always have your back." As Lila turned to leave, Serenity exhaled deeply, fortifying her resolve. She was getting closer to obtaining all the evidence she needed to dismantle and expose the lies upon which Lila had built her empire.

Chapter Three

Deception's Edge

Serenity made her way down the dimly lit corridor. The late hour ensured most of CR Enterprises' employees had long since departed, leaving the building eerily quiet. As she approached Lila's office, hushed voices caught her attention, causing her to slow her pace.

"We need to move quickly, Bradley," Lila's voice drifted through the slightly ajar door. "I need to close the Langston deal because the board is getting restless, and we can't afford any loose ends."

Serenity's breath caught in her throat. She pressed herself against the wall, her heart pounding as she strained to hear more.

Bradley's deep baritone responded, "I understand, but we have to be cautious. One wrong move and everything we've worked for could crumble."

"Don't you think I know that?" Lila hissed. "Just make sure those files disappear. Permanently."

Files? What files? Serenity fought the urge to burst into the room, instead forcing herself to remain still, gathering every scrap of information.

"Consider it done," Bradley replied, his tone resolute.

As footsteps approached the door, Serenity slipped silently into a nearby alcove, her pulse thundering in her ears. She watched as Bradley exited. Moments later, Lila emerged, her composed facade betraying nothing of the clandestine conversation.

Once alone, Serenity released a shaky breath. "Oh, Lila," she fumed. "What are you up to now?"

Pushing aside her emotions, Serenity's mind shifted into strategic mode. She needed to act fast, but carelessly rushing in would only alert

Lila to her true intentions. No, this required finesse, patience, and above all, discretion.

On her way back to her own office, Serenity suddenly changed course. She headed towards Donovan Reed's small, newly acquired office instead. The corridors seemed quieter now, stripped of the vibrancy they held when Callie ruled this domain. However, Donovan, once Callie's trusted assistant, appeared to be Serenity's best chance at uncovering the full truth.

Donovan looked up as she knocked lightly on the open door. His sharp suit belied the weariness in his eyes.

"Serenity. To what do I owe the pleasure?"

She stepped inside, closing the door behind her. They had never spoken more than a couple of words to each other in passing, so Serenity skipped the small talk and dove straight into the point. "Donovan, I believe we have a shared interest. Something mutually in common. If we team up and collaborate, we can accomplish our goals much faster."

"What can we possibly have in common?"

"I want Cartier out of prison and I'm sure you want the same for your good friend and former boss. Unless you've turned your back on Callie now that she's locked up."

His expression darkened. "Never. Go on."

"Lila is responsible for everything. Cartier is sitting in prison for crimes he didn't commit. I need to prove his innocence before it's too late."

Donovan leaned back in his chair, studying her intently. "Even after his arrest, you're still in love with him."

She didn't deny it. "Regardless of my feelings, it doesn't change the fact that he's innocent. Lila set Cartier up and Callie caught a stray bullet because she was one of his former mistresses and worked closely with him at CR Enterprises."

Donovan's eyes flickered with curiosity. "You do know that Cartier and Callie's hands aren't exactly clean?"

"If you're asking if I believe Cartier has been a Boy Scout, the answer is no. But he did not try to murder Lila, and he did not murder Cynthia. Lila orchestrated all of it, including setting him up to take the fall for corporate espionage and racketeering."

"What do you need from me?"

"I overheard Bradley and Lila talking. She told him to get rid of some files permanently. You worked closely with Callie. Do you recall anything—a conversation about documents, perhaps something Callie disregarded because she believed Lila was dead, so it was of no importance?"

Donovan sighed, running a hand through his neatly styled hair. "I'll see what I can dig up. But you need to be careful, Serenity. If everything you're saying is true, Lila doesn't just destroy her enemies; she obliterates them."

Rain pattered softly against the windows of the small diner, casting shimmering reflections of neon lights onto the wet pavement. Serenity slid into the booth where Donovan waited, his expression shadowed with a mixture of concern and determination.

"I found something," he said without preface, sliding a small key across the table. "Callie's storage unit. She kept everything there. Journals, files, records. If there's a paper trail, it's in that unit."

Serenity's fingers brushed the key, her heartbeat accelerating. "Did anyone else know about it?"

Donovan shook his head. "Callie was paranoid, especially after Lila's 'death.' She trusted no one but me. But if Lila catches wind of this…"

"She won't," Serenity interrupted, her tone firm. "I'll be careful."

Donovan hesitated. "Based on everything you told me earlier today; you do realize how dangerous Lila can be. She has no qualms about eliminating anyone she sees as a threat. Be smart about this, Serenity. If anything feels off, walk away."

Serenity pocketed the key, her willpower strengthening. "Thank you, Donovan. I won't let Lila win."

Donovan watched her leave; a sense of uneasiness crossed his face. He knew Serenity was walking a razor's edge, but he also knew there was no stopping her now. She was determined to see this through—no matter the cost.

The dim light of dawn was beginning to creep over the horizon as Serenity stood before the storage unit. The key Donovan had given her felt heavy in her hand, a tangible representation of the answers—and dangers—that awaited inside.

She scanned the area, ensuring she wasn't being followed. The facility was eerily quiet, with only the faint hum of a distant generator disturbing the silence. Serenity inserted the key into the lock, her pulse quickening as the mechanism clicked open.

Sliding the metal door upward, she was met with rows of neatly stacked boxes and a single filing cabinet. The scent of stale air and dust tickled her nose. Pulling on a pair of gloves, Serenity began her search.

Her eyes immediately landed on a box labeled *Correspondence*. She opened it carefully, rifling through envelopes, handwritten notes, and emails Callie had printed out. Her breath caught when she uncovered a letter addressed to Callie, signed with Lila's initials.

The note was brief but incriminating: *"Ensure Cartier doesn't see the LLC accounts. Burn all traces. LR."*

Serenity's hands trembled as she photographed the letter with her phone. It wasn't a smoking gun, but it was a critical piece of the puzzle. She moved to the filing cabinet, unlocking the drawers one by one. Among the meticulously filed documents, a folder labeled *Obsidian* caught her attention. Serenity's heart raced as she flipped through spreadsheets showing money transfers, many of which linked back to accounts overseas. The offshore shell corporations were all under aliases Lila had used.

Then she found it—an audio recorder tucked in the back of the drawer. Her curiosity piqued; Serenity pressed play. The muffled voices of Callie and Lila filled the storage unit.

"I told you to keep your distance from Cartier!" Lila's voice was threatening and authoritative.

"And I told you I handle my own relationships. He trusts me," Callie retorted.

"You're a liability," Lila snapped. "One misstep and this entire operation unravels. Remember, Callie, I don't just clean up messes—I erase them."

Serenity's blood ran cold. She pocketed the recorder and the *Obsidian* folder, knowing this evidence was too important to leave behind.

As she sealed the boxes and shut the cabinet, the faint sound of footsteps reached her ears. Serenity froze, her heart hammering in her chest. She turned off her flashlight and slipped into the shadows, clutching the recorder tightly.

The storage unit door rattled, then slid open further. Two figures stepped inside, silhouetted against the dim light of the hallway. Serenity's breath caught as she recognized Lila's unmistakable voice.

"Someone has been here," Lila said coldly. "Find out who and what they took."

Serenity's heart was thudding in her chest as she silently edged toward the rear exit of the unit. Every step was deliberate, her movements as quiet as possible. As the two figures began searching the boxes, she slipped out into the corridor and made her way to the parking lot.

Luckily, she parked her car just beyond the gate, out of view. Serenity moved quickly but cautiously. The moment she reached the driver's seat and locked the doors, her adrenaline surged. She started the car and sped away.

Back in the safety of her apartment, Serenity

spread the documents across her dining table. The audio recording, the letter, and the financial spreadsheets painted a clear picture: Lila had masterminded Cartier's downfall and orchestrated the cover-up with surgical precision.

But it wasn't sufficient. A skilled, high-powered attorney could easily find loopholes and redirect blame away from Lila. Serenity needed irrefutable proof to exonerate Cartier and expose Lila's schemes. And she needed to do it before Lila realized just how close she was to unraveling her empire.

Serenity picked up her phone and dialed Donovan. "I need to ask you a question. Would Callie ever join forces with Lila to take Cartier down?"

"Hell no! Never. Callie was completely in love with Cartier. Stuck on stupid. There were countless times I tried to get her to detox from that man, but he was like her drug."

"Well, in Callie's storage unit, I found indisputable proof that she was conspiring with Lila," Serenity informed him.

"What? You're positive?" he was not convinced.

"Yes. I have an audio recording."

"There must be more to it. You can't fake the

type of obsession Callie had for Cartier," Donovan insisted.

After ending the call, Serenity's mind was in turmoil. She couldn't make sense of the conflicting information she had just received - Callie's love for Cartier versus the damning audio recording that seemed to show her plotting with Lila to bring him down. But Serenity knew she couldn't let these revelations distract her from her goal: taking down Lila and clearing Cartier's name. No matter what surprises came her way, she was determined to see justice served and get revenge for all the destruction Lila had caused.

Chapter Four

Beneath the Surface

Serenity was about to get into her car, preparing for her commute to work, when Donovan's name flashed on her phone. Curious, she answered, "Hey, what's going on?"

"Meet me at the cafe by the office," Donovan said. "I did some digging of my own after our conversation last night. I want to give you what I have on Callie."

Serenity's stomach twisted in knots as she pushed the button on the console to start the engine. "I'm on the way," she exhaled.

A short while later, Serenity was at the cafe sitting across from Donovan. He slid a manila folder across the table. "I have a key to Callie's condo. I went over there this morning trying to find evidence that matched what you revealed to me last night. She has clearly always been wary of Lila, even before her supposed 'death.'"

Serenity opened the folder, her eyes scanning a series of handwritten notes, emails, and receipts. One stood out immediately: a receipt for a safe deposit box, registered under an alias Callie frequently used.

"This could be it," Serenity said anxiously. "Whatever's in that box might explain why Callie was."

Donovan nodded. "The bank is uptown. I can pull some strings to get us access, but it won't be easy."

Serenity closed the folder, her determination hardening.

"Do it. The truth is worth the risk."

Two hours later, Serenity and Donovan stood in a

private viewing room at the bank. The metal box sat on the table before them, its presence almost ominous. Donovan's contact had come through, granting them access under the guise of routine maintenance.

Serenity lifted the lid. Inside was a stack of documents and a single photograph. She picked up the photo, her breath halting. It was a candid snapshot of Callie and Lila, their smiles bright and sincere. Serenity's blood ran cold. The picture was old. Back around the time she and Lila were teenagers and in foster care together.

"She's been manipulating everyone from the start," Serenity whispered.

"I had no idea Callie knew Lila back when they were teenagers," Donovan stated, studying the photo. His brow furrowed as his eyes shifted to the documents in front of him. "Look at this," he said, holding up a notarized agreement. "Callie signed over her shares of CR Enterprises to Lila six months before Lila's 'death.'"

Serenity's thoughts were spinning. "When exactly did Lila begin to orchestrate everything?" She wondered out loud. "Was this ever about revenge and survival, or was it about control?"

"Whatever it was about, she's gotten away with it," Donovan added grimly.

"Not for much longer," Serenity replied, her voice steely. "The walls are closing in on Lila."

Serenity leaned back in the leather chair; her eyes unfocused as she stared at the sleek lines of her computer screen. The hum of the office faded away as her mind drifted to the photo she found of Callie and Lila. Then her thoughts shifted to Cartier. His face materialized in her mind—those piercing brown eyes that once looked at her with such warmth, now clouded with suspicion and betrayal.

"What have I done to us, Cartier?" she whispered, her fingers absently tracing the edge of her desk. The guilt of betraying him weighed heavily on her. A complex tangle of emotions she couldn't quite unravel.

Memories flooded back—stolen moments of passion, endless nights of making love, the kinetic intensity that always simmered between them. Serenity closed her eyes, allowing herself a moment of vulnerability.

"I'm doing this for you," she murmured, "but also for justice. For the truth."

Her daydreaming was interrupted by a sharp knock. Serenity's eyes snapped open, her mask of composure sliding back into place as she called out, "Come in."

The door opened, revealing Lila—poised, elegant, and utterly oblivious to the storm brewing beneath Serenity's calm exterior.

"Serenity, I need you to join me for a meeting with Bradley," Lila stated tersely. "We have some... delicate matters to discuss."

Serenity nodded, rising from her chair. "Of course, Lila. I'm right behind you."

As they walked down the corridor, Serenity observed Lila's confident stride, the subtle way she commanded attention without even trying. It was a striking indication of just how formidable an opponent she truly was.

They entered the conference room where Bradley waited, his expression a careful blend of professionalism and underlying anxiousness. Serenity took her seat, her senses on high alert.

Lila settled into her seat at the head of the table, her gaze sweeping over Serenity with that ever-present air of authority. Bradley leaned back slightly, his eyes darting between the two women, sensing the tension crackling in the room like electricity.

"Thank you both for joining me," Lila began, in her seamlessly smooth tone. "As you know, our upcoming gala is crucial for CR Enterprises. It is not just a social event but an opportunity to showcase our strength and influence in Atlanta's high society."

Serenity nodded, her mind working overtime to decipher Lila's true intentions. This wasn't just about a gala; it was a chess move in a much larger game.

"I trust that both of you understand the importance of this event," Lila continued, her serene facade never faltering. "We must ensure that everything runs smoothly and that our guests leave with a favorable impression of our company."

Bradley interjected cautiously, "Of course, Lila, but I must raise a concern regarding the security detail. With recent developments, I believe it would be prudent to increase surveillance and vetting of all attendees."

Serenity noticed a subtle shift in Bradley's demeanor, a flicker of nervousness hidden behind his composed exterior. She knew that he was aware of the intricate web of deception that

Lila had spun, but like her, he played his part meticulously.

Lila's demeanor remained unchanged; her expression unruffled as she regarded Bradley with a knowing look. "I appreciate your diligence, Bradley," her voice carrying a note of finality. "I have already taken steps to ensure the safety and integrity of our guests. Rest assured; everything is under control."

Lila's gaze lingered on Serenity, a subtle challenge in her eyes. "And what about you, Serenity? Do you have any insights or suggestions to ensure the gala's success?"

Serenity met Lila's glare head-on, her own eyes reflecting unyielding resolve. "I believe we should focus on highlighting our commitment to excellence and innovation. Perhaps showcasing some of our upcoming projects to demonstrate our forward-thinking approach."

Lila's smile was tight, but she nodded in agreement. "An excellent suggestion, Serenity. Bradley, I trust you will coordinate with the team to make this happen."

As the meeting progressed, Serenity sensed Lila's calculating gaze fixed on her, as if trying to discern whether she was ally or adversary. She needed to be cautious with Lila, as she was shrewd and full of surprises. It was still difficult for Serenity to grasp that she and Callie had known each other since their teenage years. She contemplated if their shared past might hold the key to unraveling all of Lila's secrets.

The Past...

Chapter Five

The Bond That Shaped Us

Years before Serenity found herself entangled in Lila's web of deceit; the two girls had shared a different life altogether. Serenity could still recall the creak of the wooden floors in the old foster home, the smell of lavender laundry detergent, and the sound of Lila's laughter, a rare and precious melody in a world that often felt cold and indifferent.

Lila had been more than just a friend to Serenity; she had been a savior, a mentor, and a sister. Four years older, Lila had a natural confidence that Serenity always admired. She carried herself with an air of defiance, her head held high no matter how bleak their circumstances seemed. Serenity clung to that strength like a lifeline.

"One day, we're going to get out of here," Lila had whispered one night, her voice filled with quiet determination. The two of them were huddled under a single blanket, the dim glow of a streetlamp seeping through the tattered curtains. "And when we do, we're going to make something of ourselves. No one will ever look down on us again."

Those words had stayed with Serenity, shaping her resolve to rise above her circumstances. She had idolized Lila, striving to emulate her boldness and resilience. But there was a side of Lila that Serenity hadn't fully understood back then—a side that was capable of keeping secrets.

It was during their teenage years that the first cracks in their bond began to form. Serenity was still navigating the complexities of entering high school and the unrelenting challenges of foster care. Lila was on the cusp of aging out of the system. She had taken on a protective role, ensuring Serenity stayed out of trouble, but she had also begun spending more time away from the foster home.

"Where do you go all the time?" Serenity had asked one evening, her tone tinged with both curiosity and concern. Lila had merely smiled, ruffling Serenity's hair in a way that was both affectionate and dismissive.

"Don't worry about it, little sis," Lila had replied. "I'm just making moves. For both of us."

What Serenity didn't know at the time was that Lila had met Callie during one of her many absences. The two had crossed paths at a youth shelter downtown, where Callie had been volunteering. Lila was drawn to Callie's charm and ambition, qualities that mirrored her own. Their connection had been immediate, and it wasn't long before they began spending time together regularly.

For Lila, Callie represented an opportunity to expand her horizons, to align herself with someone who could match her wit and drive. But their burgeoning friendship was something Lila chose to keep hidden from Serenity. Whether it was to protect her younger "sister" or to shield her from the challenges of her growing ambitions, Lila never said.

Callie's influence on Lila was profound. Under her guidance, Lila began to shed the rough edges of her foster care upbringing. Callie introduced her to a world of refinement and sophistication, teaching her everything from fashion and etiquette to how to navigate social circles with poise and grace. Lila soaked it all in, her natural charisma and intelligence amplifying the lessons Callie imparted.

Gone were the days of torn jeans and hand-me-down sneakers. Lila began wearing tailored dresses, her hair always flawlessly styled, her nails neatly polished. Although young, she was a fast learner. She quickly perfected how to command a room with her presence, her words measured and deliberate, her demeanor calm and composed. It was as if she had been reborn, emerging as a woman who could seamlessly blend into high society.

It was during this transformation that Lila caught the attention of Cartier Richardson. Their paths crossed at an exclusive charity gala; one Lila had attended as Callie's guest. Cartier, known for his discerning eye and preference for polished, demure women, was immediately captivated by Lila's elegance and charm. She was unlike anyone he had ever met—beautiful, intelligent, and enigmatic.

Lila played the part perfectly, her years of practice with Callie serving her well. She knew how to flatter without fawning, how to intrigue without revealing too much. Cartier was smitten, and Lila knew exactly how to reel him in. She had transformed herself into the idyllic partner for a man like him, leaving no trace of the rough-around-the-edges foster kid she had once been.

As the months passed, Lila's physical transformation was undeniable, but soon Serenity also noticed subtle changes in Lila's behavior. She became more secretive, her comings and goings more erratic. The once unshakable bond they had shared began to feel strained, though Serenity couldn't pinpoint why. She continued to chalk it up to Lila's impending departure from the foster system, a change she dreaded more than anything.

"What's wrong with you lately?" Serenity had finally confronted her one night, frustration bubbling to the surface. "You're always disappearing, and when you're here, it's like you're not even present."

Lila had sighed, her expression a mix of guilt and exasperation. "I'm doing what I have to do, Serenity. For both of us. You'll understand someday."

But Serenity hadn't understood. Not then. She had felt abandoned, left in the shadows of Lila's mysterious new life. Then one day Lila vanished, leaving Serenity alone in foster care. She was devastated not knowing what had happened to her best friend...her sister. She hadn't heard a word about Lila until one day she received a phone call from Cynthia, explaining that their mutual friend had been murdered, and she needed her help to expose the man who was responsible.... Lila's husband.

After Lila's supposed "death," Serenity finally discovered the truth about her relationship with Callie. Going through old records and piecing together fragments of Lila's past, she found mentions of Callie in journals and correspondence. The two had shared a partnership long before CR Enterprises, their connection rooted in a friendship Serenity had never known existed.

Once Lila married Cartier, her life became one of luxury and influence. She achieved everything she had once dreamed of, but her ambition was insatiable. She severed ties with most of her past, focusing entirely on solidifying her position as Cartier's wife and a key player in CR Enterprises.

It was during one of Cartier's high-profile

business trips that Lila's past resurfaced in the most unexpected way. While browsing a boutique in Paris, she saw a familiar face across the room. Callie.

The two women locked eyes, and for a moment, the years melted away. Lila approached her cautiously, unsure how Callie would react after all this time. But Callie's smile was warm, her demeanor as magnetic as ever.

"Lila," Callie said, embracing her. "It's been too long."

They spent the evening catching up, their bond rekindling effortlessly. Lila shared details of her life with Cartier, while Callie spoke of her ventures in corporate consulting. It wasn't long before Lila's mind began to spin with possibilities.

"Callie," Lila said, her tone conspiratorial. "I think there's a way for us to work together again. Something... big."

Callie's eyes sparkled with intrigue. "I'm listening."

From that moment on, the two women began to weave the web that would eventually ensnare Cartier, CR Enterprises, and anyone who stood in their way.

Serenity's discovery of this hidden alliance would become the key to unraveling the life Lila had so carefully constructed.

The realization was a bitter pill to swallow. Lila, the person Serenity had looked up to most, kept such a significant part of her life hidden. And now, that secret friendship had played a role in the tangled web of betrayal and manipulation that ensnared them all.

As Serenity sat in her apartment, staring at the documents before her, she couldn't help but wonder: Had Lila ever truly seen her as a sister? Or had she always been a pawn in Lila's grander schemes?

One thing was certain: the girl she'd idolized in that old foster home no longer existed. Lila had become someone else entirely—someone Serenity would have to bring down if she ever wanted to uncover the full truth and find justice for Cartier.

Chapter Six

Behind Bars

Cartier Richardson stared down at the cracked concrete floor of the jail cell, its grime a stark reminder of his fall from grace. The dim fluorescent light cast long shadows across his face, accentuating the hard lines etched by sleepless nights and relentless scheming. His mind raced, a whirlwind of betrayal and survival instincts colliding.

"How quickly the mighty fall," he mused, a bitter smirk playing at the corners of his mouth.

The irony wasn't lost on him—the CEO of CR Enterprises, reduced to a common criminal awaiting trial. The annual gala, once his crowning achievement, now seemed a distant memory, replaced by the looming specter of justice.

Cartier's fingers drummed an anxious rhythm on his thigh. "I've navigated worse," he reassured himself, though the tremor in his hand betrayed his uncertainty. Confined within those four walls, Cartier had nothing but time to contemplate. He thought of Serenity, and the night he proposed. Instead of getting prepared for his upcoming trial, they should be planning their dream wedding. His mind then shifted to Callie. She was also imprisoned, facing the same charges as him. He wondered if she was staying strong, or if her lawyer was trying to negotiate a plea deal on her behalf.

The sharp clang of metal against metal snapped Cartier out of his thoughts. He straightened, his hand reflexively adjusting the collar of his prison-issued jumpsuit, a faint echo of the confidence he once exuded in his bespoke suits. He rose slowly, adjusting his jumpsuit with practiced ease. The faint remnants of his old arrogance flared as he followed the guard through the dimly lit corridors. Other inmates watched him pass, their eyes filled with curiosity or disdain. He kept his gaze forward, his steps measured and methodical.

He followed the guard down the drab corridor, his footsteps heavy and deliberate. The visiting room came into view—a sterile space with rows of plexiglass dividers and bolted-down chairs. His gaze shifted, and then he saw her.

Serenity sat on the other side of the glass, her cream blazer and sleeked back ballerina bun was a striking contrast to the bleak surroundings. She met his eyes, her expression conflicted, a faint crack in her usually composed facade.

Cartier hesitated before sitting across from her, his movements restrained. He picked up the receiver slowly, his grip tightening as he raised it to his ear.

"Serenity," he said, his tone cool but laced with bitterness. "I didn't expect to see you here."

She swallowed hard, her lips pressing together. "Cartier, I appreciate you taking the time to talk to me. I wanted to come sooner, but I was overcome with guilt." She paused and put her head down before continuing. "There's something I need to tell you."

He leaned back in his chair, studying her with narrowed eyes. "I'm listening," he said calmly.

Her voice quivered as she spoke again. "I owe you an apology."

His eyebrow raised in question, but he remained silent, urging her to continue.

"I was the one who turned you in," she confessed, her words heavy with regret. "I believed Lila's accusations against you - that you tried to kill her, that you were responsible for everything. I thought I was doing the right thing. I was wrong."

A bitter smile crept across Cartier's face. "The right thing?" he repeated, his voice low and sharp. "You betrayed me and left me to rot in this place because you chose to believe Lila. Do you have any idea what that has cost me?"

"I do," Serenity murmured, tears welling up in her eyes. "I know I was wrong, Cartier. I know what she is capable of. Lila played me—she played us all. I'm so sorry."

He turned away, clenching his jaw as he struggled to contain the anger and pain raging inside him. "Sorry doesn't change the fact that I'm living my life behind bars, Serenity."

She leaned closer to the glass barrier separating them, desperation evident in her voice. "I'm doing everything in my power to fix this. I'm collecting evidence to prove Lila framed you. If I can piece it all together before your trial, we can get the charges dropped."

Cartier turned his attention to Serenity, a glimmer of hope appearing in his tough exterior. "Do you really think you can pull that off?"

"I have to," she responded with determination. "But it's risky. Lila can't know what I'm planning. No one can. She believes I am on her side, that I let you go. I need her to continue thinking that."

He studied her closely, his tone softening slightly. "And what about us, Serenity? What about the engagement ring I gave you?"

Her breath caught, and she looked down at her hands grasping the phone tighter. "I...I left it at your penthouse, Cartier. I could no longer wear it. If Lila thought I was still in love with you, she would destroy me as well. Everything I am doing is for you - for us. But I can't let her find out."

Cartier's expression hardened momentarily before a hint of vulnerability emerged. "So, I'm supposed to just sit around and wait? Keep my faith while you're playing her dangerous game?"

"Yes," Serenity said, her voice breaking. "I know it's asking a lot, but I need you to trust me. Please. I'm being cautious - extremely cautious. If

I make one mistake, she'll ruin everything. But I won't give up until you're free."

He exhaled deeply, the weight of her words settling over him. "You'd better be certain about this, Serenity. Because if things go wrong, I'll be the one left to deal with the consequences."

"I won't let that happen," she vowed, her eyes locked on his. "Just hold on a little longer, Cartier. I promise, I'll get you out of this."

For what felt like an eternity, neither spoke, the silence filled with the faint murmurs of other inmates and visitors filling the void. Finally, Cartier broke the silence with a nod and a resigned yet hopeful tone. "I'll trust you on that promise."

Serenity reached out and pressed her fingers against the cold glass, silently reassuring him. "I won't let you down."

As the guard approached to escort him back, Cartier stood, his eyes lingering on her. He didn't say goodbye—he didn't have to. There was no need for words between them; their understanding was strong enough to go unspoken.

As he walked away, Serenity remained seated, her heart pounding. She had chosen her path, and there was no turning back. She only hoped Cartier would keep the faith long enough for her to finish what she'd started.

The guard led Cartier back to his cell, the heavy metal door clanging shut behind him. Alone in the faintly lit confinement, he paced back and forth, his mind consumed by thoughts of Serenity's visit.

For hours, he replayed their conversation in his mind, wrestling with conflicting emotions. On one hand, there was a flicker of hope ignited by Serenity's vow to free him. On the other, there was a deep-seated fear of being betrayed once more, this time by the woman he loved.

As the hours stretched into the night, Cartier found himself unable to sleep. He sat on his cot, staring at the cold, concrete walls, shadows dancing across his weary face. The weight of uncertainty pressed down on him like a suffocating blanket.

In the darkness of his cell, he made a decision. If Serenity truly held the key to his freedom, he would trust her and steel himself against the turmoil of emotions. Only focusing on surviving each day in anticipation of Serenity's next move.

Days turned into weeks, the routine of confinement becoming a monotonous blur of meals, exercise in the cramped yard, and restless nights plagued by haunting dreams. Each passing moment marked by a relentless countdown to his trial date. Cartier clung to the promise Serenity had made, a fragile lifeline in the sea of uncertainty that surrounded him. But amidst the bleak existence behind bars, a glimmer of hope continued to flicker in the depths of his hardened heart.

Chapter Seven

Dangerous Games

The room was illuminated by the soft glow of candlelight, shadows dancing on the walls as their movements intensified. Their bodies glistened with sweat as Bradley and Lila moved in a synchronized dance of passion. Their hands explored each other's skin, tracing the curves and lines of their bodies.

Their eyes met, Lila's gaze blazing with desire, while Bradley's held a hint of uncertainty. The air was thick with the scents of sweat, perfume, and the musky aroma of sex. The smell of arousal filled the room, enticing and intoxicating. The glow of the bedside lamp cast soft shadows over the room, highlighting the sleek angles of Lila's body as she moved sinuously against Bradley. Their breath mingled in the charged air, each touch igniting the dangerous passion that had defined their affair.

Their breathing was labored and ragged, filling the room with a primal symphony of pleasure. The sound of skin on skin, moans and gasps, and the occasional whispered word of ecstasy create a soundtrack to their love making. The taste of each other's lips and skin lingers on their tongues, a mixture of sweetness and saltiness that only intensifies their desire. Lila's fingers dug into Bradley's back, nails lightly scraping his skin as her body arched with pleasure. To anyone else, this would have been intimacy. To Lila, it was control. To her, they were like two wild animals meeting in the jungle, engaged in a fierce battle that she would dominate and win.

When they finally collapsed against the pillows, their bodies tangled and damp with exertion, Bradley broke the silence. "You've been distracted lately," he said, his voice hoarse.

Lila's laugh was low and throaty, but her

eyes were distant as she traced a finger along his jawline. "Serenity," she admitted, her tone turning icy. "She might be a problem."

Bradley's brows furrowed in confusion, "How so?"

Lila sighed, a hint of frustration coloring her voice. "I can't shake the feeling that she knows something more than she's letting on. Or maybe I'm being paranoid," she shrugged.

Bradley's eyes narrowed. wary of Lila's manipulative tactics. He ran a hand through his hair, frustration building. "We need to keep a closer eye on her then. We can't afford any loose ends."

Lila nodded, her eyes hard and cold as she looked into Bradley's eyes. "I agree. If necessary, we'll take care of her." A brief moment of silence passed. "But then again, my doubts may be unfounded. I've known Serenity since we were children, and she has always been fiercely loyal. She wouldn't betray me, even if she still harbored feelings for Cartier," Lila rationalized.

A sense of unease settled over Bradley as he observed Lila, her sharp calculating gaze locking onto him with an intensity that seemed to tighten like a vice around his nerves. He had always been drawn to her power and determination, but in that moment, a seed of doubt crept into his mind. Could he truly trust Lila to protect their interests, or was he just another pawn in her intricate game?

As they lay entwined in the aftermath of their passion, the room fell into an oppressive silence broken only by the sound of their breathing. Each lost in their own thoughts, grappling with the complexities of their entangled lives and the dangers that potentially lurked ahead.

Lila finally cut through the stillness her voice soft and seductive. "Don't worry, Bradley," she said, running a hand through his hair. "I know what I'm doing. You've seen how ruthless I can be when it comes to getting what I want. Serenity won't be a problem. She's proven how devoted she is to me. However, if I'm wrong, we'll handle it like we've handled everything else."

Bradley nodded, trying to quell the unease that still lingered within him. He knew he had to trust Lila, but he couldn't help feeling like they were on a dangerous tightrope walk, with one false move sending them plummeting into the abyss.

Chapter 8

Corporate Espionage

The sleek glass doors of CR Enterprises parted before Serenity Clayborn like a curtain rising on a high-stakes performance. She strode into the lobby, her blush-colored Louboutin pumps clicking purposefully across the marble floor. The atrium soared above her, its modern elegance a fitting stage for the corporate power plays about to unfold.

Serenity's mind raced, analyzing every variable, every potential pitfall in her carefully orchestrated plan. As she approached Audra was speaking with her assistant Reese. Their eyes met. Audra's lips curved in the barest hint of a smile, a subtle signal that set Serenity's pulse quickening.

It's on, Serenity thought, returning Audra's look with a nearly imperceptible nod.

"Good morning, Ms. Clayborn," Reese chirped, her tone cheery but eyes glinting with shared purpose. "Mrs. Richardson is expecting you."

"Thank you, Reese," Serenity replied smoothly. She paused, adjusting an imaginary wrinkle in her tailored blazer. "Any messages?"

"Nothing urgent," Reese said.

"Though Mr. Upton was asking about the quarterly projections," Audra added with a playful cadence belying the weight of their exchange.

Serenity's brow furrowed slightly. Upton's interest could complicate matters. She filed the information away, another piece in the intricate puzzle she was assembling.

"I'll follow up with him later," Serenity said, her voice steady despite the adrenaline coursing through her veins. She turned toward Lila's office, each step bringing her closer to the precipice.

Calm, she reminded herself. You've prepared for this. You know what's at stake.

The polished mahogany of Lila's door loomed before her. Serenity took a measured breath, schooling her features into a mask of professional poise. Her hand hesitated for just a moment on the handle before she pushed it open, stepping into the lion's den.

"Serenity," Lila's melodic voice greeted her. "Right on time, as always."

Serenity met Lila's gaze, taking in the other woman's impeccable appearance. Even seated behind her imposing desk, Lila radiated an aura of authority that filled the room.

"I wouldn't dream of keeping you waiting," Serenity replied, her tone warm yet carefully modulated. She settled into one of the chairs facing Lila, crossing her legs at the ankle. "I hope I'm not interrupting anything pressing?"

Lila's laugh was musical, almost hypnotic. "For you? Never. Now, tell me, how are the preparations coming along for next month's product launch?"

Serenity leaned forward slightly, her posture open and engaged. "Everything's on track," she replied, her voice smooth as silk. "The marketing team has outdone themselves with the campaign visuals. I think you'll be particularly impressed with the social media strategy we've developed."

As she spoke, Serenity calculated each word, each subtle shift in body language. She needed to appear eager, competent, but not overly so. The dance of corporate intrigue required a delicate balance.

Lila nodded; her eyes sharp. "Excellent. And the projections for Q3?"

"Looking strong," Serenity said, allowing a hint of pride to color her tone. "We're forecasting a 12% increase in revenue, primarily driven by the new luxury line."

She watched Lila carefully, searching for any flicker of reaction. Does she suspect? Serenity wondered. Or am I nothing more than a piece in her elaborate design?

"Impressive," Lila murmured, her fingers drumming lightly on the polished surface of her desk. "You've certainly proven your worth to CR Enterprises, Serenity. I hope you know how much we value your... contributions."

The pause was barely noticeable, but it sent a chill down Serenity's spine. She forced a gracious smile, even as her heart thundered in her chest.

"That means a great deal coming from you, Lila," Serenity said, her voice steady despite the tension coiling in her gut. "I'm honored to be part of the team here at CRE."

Lila's answering smile was enigmatic, a Mona Lisa curve that revealed nothing. "Well, I won't keep you any longer. I'm sure you have plenty to attend to, especially with the gala being tomorrow evening. Are you ready?"

Serenity rose, her movements fluid and unhurried. "Of course."

As she turned to leave, Serenity felt Lila's gaze boring into her back. She resisted the urge to quicken her pace, to betray any sign of the turmoil roiling beneath her calm exterior. Instead, she maintained her poised demeanor, each as she exited Lila's office.

The moment the door closed behind her; Serenity released a breath she hadn't realized she'd been holding. Her mind raced, dissecting every nuance of the conversation. What did Lila know? How much had she gleaned?

Serenity's eyes darted to Audra's desk, finding her confidante's reassuring gaze. A subtle nod passed between them, an unspoken agreement to meet later. For now, appearances had to be maintained.

As Serenity made her way across the expansive office floor, the glass walls of CR Enterprises seemed to close in around her. The sleek, modern design that once symbolized progress and ambition now felt like a gilded cage, every reflective surface a potential witness to her covert mission.

She paused at her own office door, her hand hovering over the handle. Through the glass, she could see the skyline of Atlanta sprawled before her, a testament to the power and influence of CR Enterprises. And somewhere in this concrete jungle, Cartier was waiting, counting on her to unravel the web of deceit that had ensnared him.

"Ms. Clayborn?" A junior associate's voice broke through her contemplation. "The marketing team is waiting for you in Conference Room B."

Serenity nodded, her mask of professionalism sliding effortlessly back into place. "Thank you, I'll be right there."

As she turned towards the conference room, Serenity steeled herself for the next act in this dangerous play. The stakes were higher than ever, and one false move could bring everything crashing down.

Serenity took a deep breath, straightened

her shoulders, and knocked on Lila's office door once again. The soft tap echoed in her ears like a drumbeat, signaling the start of their high-stakes encounter.

"Come in," Lila's authoritative voice rang out.

Serenity entered, her face a carefully crafted mask of deference and loyalty. Lila was still sitting behind her imposing glass desk, the Atlanta skyline framing her silhouette. Her piercing gaze locked onto Serenity, assessing and calculating.

"Serenity, back so soon. What can I do for you?" Lila's voice was disarming. But despite her pleasant tone, there was a subtle firmness. "Did we forget to cover something during our previous conversation?"

"Yes, the upcoming board meeting." Serenity replied, her voice steady despite the rush coursing through her veins. "I've been working on some projections that I believe could be beneficial."

Lila leaned back, her eyes never leaving Serenity's face. "Go on."

Serenity carefully selected each word. "I've noticed some... discrepancies in our recent financial reports. Nothing alarming, but I thought it prudent to bring them to your attention before the meeting."

A flash of something - surprise? concern? - crossed Lila's face before vanishing. "Discrepancies? Of what nature?"

"Minor inconsistencies in our offshore accounts," Serenity replied, watching Lila's reaction intently. "I'm sure it's nothing, but given the board's recent scrutiny and with you wanting to finalize the Langston deal..."

Lila's fingers drummed on the desk, a rare show of agitation. "I see. Thank you for bringing this to my attention, Serenity. I'll look into it personally."

As Serenity left Lila's office, her pulse thrumming. She had planted the seed of doubt, but at what cost? Her eyes darted to Audra's desk, catching her colleague's gaze. With a subtle nod, Serenity made her way to a secluded corner of the building, Audra following moments later.

"What did you find?" Serenity whispered, her back to the wall, eyes scanning for any potential eavesdroppers.

Audra leaned in close, her voice barely audible. "Lila's been making frequent calls to an unlisted number. I managed to trace it - it's a burner phone registered to a shell company with ties to the Peachtree Syndicate."

Serenity's blood ran cold. The pieces were

falling into place, but the picture they formed was more dangerous than she had ever imagined.

The autumn sun cast long shadows across the pristine sidewalk as Donovan adjusted his tie, his eyes scanning the bustling street outside CR Enterprises' towering headquarters. A sleek black sedan pulled up, and a distinguished man in his fifties emerged, his salt-and-pepper hair neatly combed.

"Mr. Franklin Whitaker," Donovan greeted, extending his hand. "Thank you for meeting me on such short notice."

Whitaker's grip was firm. "Anything for an old friend, Donovan. Shall we walk?"

As they strolled, Donovan's voice remained low and measured. "I need information on certain financial transactions that may have slipped under the radar."

Whitaker's eyebrow raised. "Dangerous territory, my friend. What exactly are we looking for?"

Donovan paused, weighing his words carefully. "Inconsistencies that might suggest... external influence on company decisions."

"You're dancing around something, Donovan," Whitaker observed. "Does this have to do with Callie and Cartier's current situation?"

"I can't divulge specifics, Franklin. But if what I suspect is true, the implications could be far-reaching."

Whitaker nodded slowly. "I understand. I'll see what I can dig up, but tread carefully. The waters you're wading into are deep and murky."

As they parted ways, Donovan felt a combination of relief and trepidation. He had now set the wheels in motion.

Meanwhile, in the dimly lit company archives, Serenity inserted the key Donovan had given her into the steel file cabinet, unlocking it to access the confidential files inside. Her fingers flew over documents after documents, trying to connect the dots. The faint hum of fluorescent lights provided an eerie backdrop to her clandestine search.

"There has to be something here," she muttered, pushing a stray lock of hair behind her ear. Her eyes widened as she stumbled upon a series of memos detailing unusual fund transfers. The dates aligned perfectly with Cartier's alleged misconduct, but the signatures... they didn't match his usual scrawl.

"Oh, Lila," she whispered with triumph, "I'm getting close."

A sudden echo of footsteps in the corridor jolted Serenity from her sleuthing. Her pulse quickened as the sound grew louder, each step a thunderous threat to her covert mission. With practiced efficiency, she swiftly gathered the incriminating documents, her fingers trembling slightly as she slid them into a nondescript folder.

"Calm yourself," she thought, taking a deep breath to steady her nerves.

Serenity smoothly transitioned to rifling through an innocuous stack of quarterly reports, adopting an air of casual concentration. The footsteps paused outside the archives, and she felt a bead of sweat trickle down her spine.

"Ms. Clayborn?" A voice called out, tinged with curiosity.

"In here," she responded, injecting a note of cheerful professionalism into her tone. "Just double-checking some figures for the board meeting."

As the footsteps receded, Serenity exhaled slowly. Time was slipping away like sand through an hourglass, and she needed to act swiftly.

Across the office, Audra's keen eyes scanned the bustling workspace, her vibrant auburn hair catching the light as she shifted in her chair. Her gaze settled on Bradley Upton, who was engaged in a hushed conversation on his cell phone near the elevator. Something about his body language set off alarm bells in her mind.

"Well, well, Mr. Upton," Audra mused silently, her hazel eyes narrowing. "What secrets are you trying to hide?"

She observed as Bradley glanced furtively around the lobby, his normally composed demeanor betraying a hint of agitation. His fingers drummed an erratic rhythm on his thigh, a nervous tic she'd never noticed before.

"Looks like our resident boy scout is up to no good," she thought, making a mental note to relay this information to Serenity.

As if on cue, Serenity approached, her expression a picture of calm, though a storm of thoughts raged beneath the surface. Audra caught her eye and gave an almost imperceptible nod towards Bradley.

Serenity stepped closer to Audra; her voice soft yet deliberate. "Anything interesting while I was away?"

Audra leaned in, "Oh, you know how it is. Just

another day of scheming. Although, our friend Bradley seems to be slightly rattled."

Serenity's eyebrow arched slightly. "Is that so? How... intriguing."

"Indeed, we can further discuss later," Audra replied, her eyes sparkling with mischief.

As Serenity walked away, Audra couldn't help but feel a thrill of excitement. The game was no longer on cruise control, it was speeding up, and she was right in the middle of it all.

Serenity glided into her office, the door closing behind her with a soft click. She exhaled deeply, allowing her composed façade to slip for just a moment. Her eyes darted to the hidden compartment in her desk drawer, where she'd stashed the documents, she'd unearthed in the archives.

With practiced efficiency, she retrieved the papers and spread them across her desk. Her nimble fingers traced the intricate web of connections she'd uncovered, each thread leading back to Lila's carefully constructed empire of lies.

"Oh, Lila," Serenity murmured, her voice tinged with admiration and disgust. "You've woven quite the tapestry. But every thread has its weakness."

As she pored over the documents, she deliberated how could she leverage this information without tipping her hand too soon? The stakes were too high for rash action.

Suddenly, an uninvited memory flashed in her mind's eye. Cartier's face, illuminated by candlelight, his dark eyes intense as he leaned towards her across a table at Le Bilboquet.

"Serenity," he'd said, his tone filled with urgency. "There's more at play here than you realize. Trust no one."

His warning caught her off guard, causing her to lift her glass of champagne. "Not even you, darling?"

He grinned, but his eyes remained serious. "Especially not me." Then he laughed. "I'm just teasing."

Despite his play on words, Serenity couldn't shake the feeling there was some truth behind Cartier's warning.

Serenity shook her head, dispelling the memory. That night felt like a lifetime ago, before she found out Lila was really alive, before the arrest, before everything unraveled.

"Oh, Cartier," she whispered, her fingers unconsciously tracing the outline of the key in her pocket. "What tangled web did you weave? And how do I unravel it without destroying us both?"

Chapter Nine

Cracks in the Facade

The boardroom's glass walls mirrored the expansive Atlanta skyline as Serenity entered with meticulous grace, her heels clicking steadily against the smooth marble floor. Though her heart raced, her face betrayed nothing but calm authority. "Good morning, everyone. My apologies for the delay," she said politely, offering a composed smile as she took her seat.

Lila sat at the head of the table, her posture regal, surrounded by a cadre of executives. Lila and Serenity's presence caused a palpable tension in the room, as their eyes darted back and forth between them.

"Serenity, so glad you could join us," Lila purred, her voice dripping with honey-coated venom.

Serenity took her seat, crossing her legs elegantly. "I wouldn't miss it for the world," she replied, her tone matching Lila's false warmth. She scanned the room, noting the nervous twitches and averted gazes. These men were puppets, and Lila held their strings.

"We were just discussing the Langston acquisition," Lila said, outlining her aggressive expansion strategy. Serenity plotted how to challenge without revealing her hand? She waited for her moment, then struck.

"Impressive plan, Lila," Serenity interjected, her voice full of praise. "But have you considered the potential fallout from the EU's new luxury goods regulations?"

Lila's eyes narrowed subtly. "Of course, we've factored that in."

"Have we?" Serenity pressed, leaning forward. "Because our projections seem overly optimistic given the current political climate in France."

A flicker of uncertainty crossed Lila's face, quickly replaced by edginess. "Your concern is noted, Serenity. Perhaps you'd like to present an alternative strategy at our next meeting?"

Serenity smiled, recognizing the challenge for what it was. "I am managing the account, so it would be my pleasure."

As the meeting proceeded, Serenity watched Lila closely, noting every micro expression, every slight shift in body language. She's rattled, Serenity thought. But how far can I push before she pushes back?

Once the meeting was over and the moment the boardroom door closed behind her; Serenity's composed facade cracked. She strode purposefully through the labyrinth of glass-walled offices, her mind whirling with the implications of what had just transpired.

In a secluded alcove near the fire stairs, Audra and Donovan awaited her arrival. Serenity's eyes darted left and right, ensuring their privacy before she spoke in hushed tones.

"Lila's definitely hiding something about Langston," she murmured. "She tried to brush it off, but she practically cringed when I mentioned the EU regulations."

Audra's hazel eyes glinted with excitement.

"I knew it! I overheard Bradley on the phone earlier, mentioning some sort of 'offshore arrangement.' Think it's connected?"

Donovan nodded, his expression grave. "It fits the pattern. My contact at the SEC hinted at irregularities in CRE's recent filings. If we can prove Lila's circumventing regulations..."

"We might just have her," Serenity finished, a surge of adrenaline coursing through her veins. "But we need concrete evidence. Audra, can you—"

"Already on it," Audra interjected with a sly smile. "I've got a backdoor into Bradley's email. Give me 48 hours."

Serenity turned to Donovan. "And you?"

He straightened his cufflinks, a gesture of confidence and resolve. "I'll reach out to my inside connects. If there's a paper trail, we'll find it."

"Perfect," Serenity exhaled. "I also found some useful documents in the company archives," her eyes twinkled, handing the key Donovan gave her back to him. "We're close. I can feel it." She paused, her voice softening. "Thank you both. I couldn't get any of this done without you."

Audra squeezed her arm. "We're in this together, girl. All the way."

"Great! I'll see you all tonight at the Gala," Serenity winked.

The gala that evening was a dazzling display of luxury and grandeur, with Cartier Enterprises' headquarters transformed into a radiant palace, illuminated by the glow of countless glistening lights.

Serenity moved through the crowd with effortless elegance, wearing a chic gown that shimmered like moonlit waters, the fabric cascading around her like a silken cocoon. Her dark hair was swept up in an intricate twist, strands framing her face in a soft halo. Her eyes scanning the sea of designer gowns and tailored suits for any sign of intrigue.

As she reached the grand staircase leading up to the VIP section, she spotted Audra and Donovan by the bar. Serenity made her way to them, the soft music and murmur of conversations creating a backdrop to their hushed exchange.

"Serenity, you made it," Audra exclaimed, handing her a glass of champagne.

Serenity took the glass with a mischievous smile, raising an eyebrow. "Any updates?" she inquired quietly, mindful of prying ears in the vicinity.

Audra leaned in, her voice barely above a whisper. "Bradley's emails were a goldmine. There's definitely something shady going on with Langston. I've forwarded you the details."

Serenity nodded, impressed by Audra's swift action. "And Donovan?"

Donovan chimed in; his tone serious. "I've managed to secure access to some of Lila's encrypted files. There are discrepancies that could point to financial improprieties, but we'll need to decrypt them to be sure."

Serenity nodded, "We're making progress," she said softly, a determined glint in her gaze. "Let's keep pushing forward."

As the evening wore on, Serenity mingled with the elite guests, her interactions a careful dance of charm and strategy. She exchanged pleasantries with executives and influential figures, her every move calculated and graceful, all while keeping a watchful eye on Lila.

In a secluded corner of the balcony overlooking the city lights, Serenity found herself face to face with Lila. The air between them crackled with unspoken tension as they regarded each other with cool detachment.

"Beautiful evening, isn't it?" Lila's voice was smooth, betraying none of the turmoil Serenity knew lay beneath.

Serenity nodded; her gaze unwavering. "Indeed, a perfect backdrop for unexpected revelations," she remarked before becoming distracted by the unfolding drama below. She stood motionless on the balcony, her manicured fingers gripping the ornate railing as her gaze remained fixed. Beside her, Lila mirrored her stance, their silent communication conveyed through the subtlest of glances.

A faint crease appeared between Serenity's brows as she observed Bradley Upton, his usually composed demeanor cracking under the pressure of the confrontation. The mysterious man loomed before him, an ominous presence in the midst of the glittering gala. Bradley's voice, taut with barely contained fury, carried up to the balcony. "You have no right to make such demands. We had an agreement and CR Enterprises has held up its end."

The mysterious man's response was low, menacing. "Agreements are flexible for those you know how to bend for, Mr. Upton. Surely, you understand that by now."

Bradley's words were laced with defiance. "Our arrangement has limits. You're overstepping."

"Limits?" the man's laughter was cold, devoid of humor. "The Peachtree Syndicate recognizes no limits, especially not those imposed by men who forget their place."

Serenity's fingers tightened on the railing. She could almost feel the tension radiating from Bradley, his carefully constructed world threatening to unravel before her eyes. What secrets lay buried beneath this confrontation? And how could she use this newfound knowledge to her advantage?

As the heated exchange continued, Serenity's mind whirred with possibilities. The pieces of the puzzle were slowly falling into place, revealing a picture far more complex and treacherous than she had initially imagined.

The mysterious man's demeanor remained unnervingly placid, a stark contrast to the heated exchange. His eyes, cold and calculating, never left Bradley's face. As he shifted his weight, the dim light caught a flash of gold on his lapel - a stylized peach blossom, the unmistakable emblem of the Peachtree Syndicate.

"Mr. Upton," he said, continuing his menacing purr, "surely you understand the... delicate nature of our arrangement." His fingers traced the emblem absently, a gesture that seemed almost unconscious but carried the weight of unspoken threats.

Bradley's response was cut short as a looming presence materialized beside the mysterious man. The bodyguard, a behemoth of a man, stood with arms crossed, his very stillness radiating danger. Muscles rippled beneath his tailored suit, hinting at barely contained violence.

Serenity felt her breath catch. The subtle interplay of power before her was as fascinating as it was terrifying. She couldn't help but wonder, 'How deep does this web of influence extend?'

The bodyguard's eyes, dark and alert, scanned the surroundings ceaselessly. When they briefly met Serenity's gaze, she felt a chill run down her spine. In that moment, she knew - one wrong move, and this man could snap a life as easily as a twig.

Bradley's jaw clenched, a muscle twitching beneath his usually composed exterior. His fingers curled into fists at his sides, knuckles whitening as he fought to maintain his stance.

"Our arrangement," he said, voice low and

strained, "was never meant to compromise the integrity of CR Enterprises." Bradley's eyes darted briefly to the looming bodyguard before returning to the mysterious man's face.

The man's lip curled into a sardonic smile. "Integrity? You no longer have none. You sold it, remember, Mr. Upton."

Bradley's mind was spinning. How had he allowed himself to become entangled in this web? The weight of his choices pressed down on him, threatening to crack his carefully constructed facade.

"We can discuss this like civilized—" Bradley began, but his words were cut short as the bodyguard suddenly surged forward.

A meaty fist connected with Bradley's solar plexus, driving the air from his lungs. He doubled over, gasping, as the behemoth followed through with a vicious uppercut that snapped Bradley's head back.

Onlookers erupted into a chaotic symphony of shocked gasps and startled cries. Bradley staggered, vision blurring, tasting copper in his mouth. His analytical mind, usually so sharp, struggled to process the sudden violence.

'This can't be happening,' 'Not here, not now,' Bradley thought desperately, even as he felt himself falling. The marble floor rushed to meet him, cold and unforgiving.

Lila's eyes narrowed, surveying the scene. This wasn't just an assault on Bradley; it was an affront to everything CR Enterprises represented. She turned to leave her voice a low, controlled fury.

"This must be handled. Now!"

Serenity nodded sharply, turning towards Lila but she had disappeared. Serenity saw a security officer barking orders into a concealed earpiece.

Within moments, a team of black-suited security personnel materialized, their movements precise and coordinated. They formed a protective circle around Bradley, who was struggling to his feet with Reese's assistance.

"Clear the area!" The lead security officer's voice brooked no argument. "Please remain calm and step back."

While the crowd reluctantly retreated, Serenity watched as the security team led the mysterious man and his imposing bodyguard towards the exit, he turned, his eyes locking onto Bradley with predatory intensity. The room fell silent, hanging on his every word.

"Remember, Mr. Upton," he said, his voice

carrying a haunting omen, "the Peachtree Syndicate doesn't make idle threats. Your time is running out."

Bradley's face paled, completely defeated. He opened his mouth to retort, but only a strained whisper escaped. "You don't understand what you're dealing with."

The mysterious man's lips curled into a cold smile. "Oh, I think we do. And soon, so will everyone else."

As he was escorted out, Bradley slumped against a nearby pillar, his breathing ragged. The implications of the threat hung heavy in the air, leaving the gala attendees in stunned silence.

Bradley's hand trembled as he reached for a glass of champagne, nearly knocking it over before grasping it tightly. He took a long swallow, adam's apple bobbing as he fought to regain his composure.

High above, on the balcony overlooking the scene, Serenity wondered about the potential fallout from this very public disturbance. Her investigative gaze swept over the display. Her delicate features betrayed nothing, but her mind raced, assessing every nuance of the confrontation.

"This changes the landscape," Audra said,

her fingers tightening around her champagne flute, focusing on Bradley's shaken form.

Serenity turned and saw Audra and Donovan standing behind her, both quiet, deep in thought. She closed the distance between them, the soft rustle of her gown punctuating the eerie silence. "Yes, it does."

"The Syndicate's boldness... it's unexpected," Donovan observed.

"And dangerous," Serenity added, a silent challenge in her eyes. "We'll need to accelerate our timeline. If the Syndicate is making such public moves..." She trailed off, leaving the implications unspoken.

Moments later, Lila stepped back onto the balcony, her composed exterior untouched. The two women exchanged a loaded glance heavy with unspoken words. Years of shared history and concealed motives hung between them as a silent understanding passed. Their actions moved in unison, an uncanny ballet of secrecy and calculated intent.

The Past...

Chapter Ten

Shadows of the Past

Sunlight dappled the lush garden, casting a golden glow on two young girls as they chased each other through a maze of rosebushes. Serenity's carefree laughter rang out, her dark curls bouncing as she ducked behind a fragrant bloom. Lila's eyes sparkled with mischief as she lunged forward, her fingertips grazing Serenity's sleeve.

"Got you!" Lila exclaimed, triumphant.

Serenity spun around, her chest heaving

with exertion and joy. "You're too fast for me, Lila. How do you always catch me?"

As they collapsed onto the soft grass, their giggles subsided into contented sighs. Serenity marveled at how effortlessly Lila moved, her grace apparent even in childhood games. A warm breeze rustled the leaves above, and Serenity felt a sudden urge to share her innermost thoughts.

"Let's go to our special spot," she whispered, tugging Lila's hand.

They scampered towards an ancient oak tree, its gnarled branches offering a canopy of secrecy. Settling into a nook formed by twisted roots, Serenity leaned close to Lila, their shoulders touching.

"I had a dream last night," Serenity confided, her voice barely above a whisper. "I was standing on top of a huge building, looking down at the whole city. Everything seemed so small, but I felt... powerful."

Lila's eyes widened with intrigue. "What did you do up there?"

Serenity paused, struggling to articulate the emotions that had surged through her in the dream. "I wanted to make things right. To fix all the unfairness in the world."

A shadow of understanding flickered across Lila's face. "That sounds amazing, Serenity. I bet you could do it, too. You always know how to make things fair when we play."

Serenity's heart swelled with her friend's faith in her. She wondered if Lila ever had such grand visions for herself. "What about you, Lila? What do you dream about?"

Lila's gaze turned distant, her voice taking on a quiet intensity. "I want to be strong enough to protect the people I care about. To make sure no one can ever hurt us."

The words hung in the air, heavy with unspoken meaning. Serenity felt a shiver of premonition, sensing the steel beneath Lila's gentle exterior. She reached out, intertwining her fingers with Lila's.

"We'll always protect each other," Serenity declared, her young voice filled with conviction. "No matter what happens, we'll stick together."

Lila squeezed her hand, a small smile playing at the corners of her mouth. "Always, Serenity. You and me against the world."

As they sat in companionable silence, Serenity's mind raced with possibilities. She imagined herself and Lila, grown and powerful, standing atop that skyscraper from her dream.

The thought both thrilled and unsettled her, a glimpse of a future yet to be written.

The tranquil moment shattered as a harsh voice cut through the air. "Lila! Serenity! Get in here, now!"

Serenity winced, her hand tightening instinctively around Lila's. Their foster mother, Mrs. Hawkins, stood on the back porch, her face twisted in a scowl.

"Coming, Mrs. Hawkins," Lila called out, her voice steady despite the sudden tension in her shoulders.

As they approached, Serenity could smell the sour tang of alcohol on Mrs. Hawkins' breath. The woman's eyes narrowed, focusing on Lila.

"You ungrateful little brat," Mrs. Hawkins spat. "I saw you sneaking food from the pantry. Think you can steal from me?"

Lila stood tall; her chin lifted. "I didn't steal anything, Mrs. Hawkins. Serenity and I were hungry, and you hadn't made dinner yet."

Serenity's heart raced. She wanted to speak up, to defend Lila, but fear kept her silent. Instead, she watched in awe as her friend faced down their foster mother.

Mrs. Hawkins lunged forward, grabbing Lila's arm. "Don't you dare talk back to me!"

"Let go," Lila said, her voice low and dangerous. "You're hurting me."

Serenity's mind whirled. How could Lila be so brave? She thought, I wish I could be that strong.

As Mrs. Hawkins raised her hand, Lila twisted free, her eyes flashing. "Touch me again, and I'll report you. I know your dirty little secrets."

The threat hung in the air, electric. Mrs. Hawkins paled, taking a step back.

"Get out of my sight," she hissed. "Both of you."

As they hurried away, Serenity whispered, "That was amazing, Lila. How did you do that?"

Lila's expression was grim. "Sometimes you have to fight fire with fire, Serenity. Come on, I know a place we can go."

The girls slipped out of the house, their footsteps quick and light on the cracked sidewalk. Serenity's heart still pounded from the confrontation, but a thrill of excitement coursed through her veins as they ventured into the fading afternoon light.

"Where are we going?" Serenity asked, her voice hushed.

Lila's eyes gleamed with mischief. "You'll see. Trust me."

They wound their way through the neighborhood, past overgrown lots and boarded-up houses. Finally, Lila stopped in front of a dilapidated Victorian, its paint peeling and windows dark.

"This is it," Lila announced. "Our secret hideout."

Serenity hesitated. "Are you sure it's safe?"

Lila squeezed her hand. "We're safer here than back there. Come on."

They crept around to the back, where Lila expertly jimmied open a loose board. As they slipped inside, dust motes danced in the slanting sunlight. The air was thick with the scent of decay and forgotten dreams. "Wow," Serenity breathed, taking in the grand staircase and chandelier, now cobweb-draped and tarnished.

Lila grinned. "It's like our own little kingdom, isn't it?"

As they explored, Serenity's unease melted away, replaced by a sense of an eerie adventure. The floorboards creaked ominously beneath their feet as Serenity and Lila ventured deeper into the abandoned house's shadowy interior. Floating debris swirled in the faint beams of light streaming through the gaps in the boarded-up windows, casting an otherworldly glow that sent a chill down Serenity's spine.

"Look at this," Serenity whispered, her fingers tracing the outline of a peculiar seam in the wall. With a gentle push, a hidden panel swung open, revealing a small compartment. "Lila, come here!"

Lila approached cautiously, her eyes narrowing as Serenity reached into the darkness. "Be careful, Serenity. We don't know what's in there."

Serenity's hand grasped something solid, and she pulled it out slowly to reveal a book. It was a journal with elegant cursive handwriting filling each page. "There are so many words," she remarked as she gazed at the pages. "I wonder who wrote it?" She turned the journal over in her hand, examining it closely.

Lila's finger traced a few lines of faded ink as she turned the pages "We should head back to the house and read this before it gets too dark. I don't want to deal with Mrs. Hawkins' mouth," Lila retorted with disdain.

The two girls raced out of the abandoned house, eager to see what secrets were hidden inside the leather journal.

After returning from their peaceful exploration, they settled on the front porch to start reading through the journal. Suddenly, a loud crash in the distance shook them both. Serenity's heart leapt into her throat as muffled shouting filtered through the door.

"That's coming from the house," Lila hissed, her playful demeanor evaporating.

They crept towards a filthy window, peering inside their foster home. Through the window, they could see their foster father, red-faced and bellowing, hurling a plate against the wall. Their foster mother cowered; arms raised defensively.

Serenity's breath caught. "We have to do something!"

Lila grabbed her arm, eyes flashing with a determination Serenity had never seen before. "No. We have to leave. Now."

"But—"

"Listen to me," Lila's voice was low, intense. "This is our chance. We go back to the group home, together. We protect each other. Always."

The sounds of breaking glass and terrified sobbing pierced the air. Serenity was torn between the instinct to help and the desperate need to escape. She looked at Lila, saw the courage in her friend's gaze, and made her choice.

"Okay," Serenity whispered, her voice trembling. "Together."

Lila pulled Serenity into a gentle embrace. "Hey, look at me. We've got each other, okay? No matter what happens, I'll always have your back. We're stronger together."

Serenity leaned into the comfort of her friend's arms, feeling the steady rhythm of Lila's heartbeat. "I'm scared sometimes," she admitted. "About the future, about what might happen to us."

"It's okay to be scared," Lila murmured, her fingers combing through Serenity's hair. "But remember, fear can make us cautious, and caution can keep us safe. We'll face whatever comes our way, just like we always have."

She looked at Lila, who was like her big sister, her best friend, and protector, and knew that whatever came, they would face it together.

Lila gripped Serenity's arm as she pulled her away from the window. "We grab what we can and go. Don't look back."

They managed to slip in through the back door, hastily throwing their belongings into a bag before being seen by their foster parents. Then they ran, hand in hand, leaving behind the cacophony of violence and the shattered remnants of what should have been a home. The world suddenly seemed darker, more dangerous, but

Serenity clung to one comforting thought: she and Lila had each other, and together, they would survive.

Once they had escaped from their foster parents and returned to the group home, Lila and Serenity waited until the late evening to quietly slip out and head to the park. In that moment, it was as if nothing had changed. They both gazed up at the beautiful stars in the sky above, finding solace in each other's presence just like they always did in the past.

As they looked up bathed in the starlight, the stars remained silent, but their steady presence offered a strange comfort. Serenity's musing was abruptly interrupted by an icy shiver. Her eyes widened as a dark shadow crept across the face of the moon, its edges sharp and ominous.

"Lila," she whispered, an inexplicable sense of dread gripping her heart.

The park, once peaceful, now seemed fraught with unseen dangers. The rustling of leaves sounded almost like whispered conspiracies.

Serenity stood, "I'm ready to head back. For some reason I'm getting a creepy feeling out here," she sighed. The shadow slow crawled across the moon, casting an eerie grayness over the landscape.

"We can go," Lila said taking Serenity's hand.

With one last look at the veiled moon, Serenity turned and began to walk home with Lila. The park gates creaked shut behind them, a haunting reminder: innocence, like the moonlight, can be stolen in an instant.

Chapter Eleven

The Trial Begins

The mahogany doors of Courtroom 12 swung open with an ominous creak, unleashing a wave of hushed whispers that rippled through the gallery. Rich with confidence and a hint of challenge, Cartier stood buttoning his designer suit jacket with a fluid motion. Judge Eliza Hargrove's gavel cracked against the sound block, silencing the murmurs as effectively as a gunshot.

"You may be seated. The People versus Cartier Richardson and Callie Morgan will now commence."

Cartier's fingers tightened imperceptibly on the polished edge of the defense table, his expression a mask of cool composure. He surveyed the jury box, noting the mix of curiosity and wariness etched on their faces. A middle-aged woman with graying hair caught his eye, her brow furrowed in concentration. Potential ally or adversary? He mused, cataloging her reaction for future reference.

As the clerk read out the charges—racketeering, money laundering, conspiracy—Cartier allowed his gaze to drift across the courtroom. The prosecutors, one an older silver haired gentleman, the other a sharp-eyed woman in a crisp navy suit, who was arranging her notes with practiced precision. The jury leaned forward, fully engaged.

Cartier's hand moved to his tie, adjusting the Windsor knot with a practiced motion that belied the sudden quickening of his pulse. He turned, meeting Callie's eyes for the briefest of moments.

Cartier perused the room, dissecting every detail. The USB drive weighed heavily in his memory, its contents a ticking time bomb that could shatter everything he'd built. But he'd faced worse odds before, clawed his way up from nothing to stand atop Atlanta's impressive social hierarchy.

Cartier continued to keep his eyes locked on the jury. Let the games begin, he thought. This was just another boardroom, another negotiation, and Cartier Richardson didn't lose.

Callie Morgan sat beside Cartier, her posture a study in elegant defiance. Her eyes, sharp as cut emeralds, swept the courtroom with predatory intensity. Each juror, each spectator, each potential threat catalogued and assessed in a heartbeat.

"Quite the crowd," she murmured, her voice low enough for only Cartier to hear. "Atlanta's finest, come to watch us fall."

Cartier's lips quirked in a barely perceptible smirk. "They'll be sorely disappointed," he commented, as the prosecutor began her opening statement.

The sharp-featured woman with steely eyes, rose to her feet. "Your Honor, members of the jury," she began, her voice cutting through the hushed courtroom, "the evidence will show that Cartier Richardson and Callie Morgan have systematically defrauded investors and manipulated markets for their own gain while also committing a heinous murder."

Callie forcefully pressed the pen down on a notepad releasing her immediate frustration. The prosecutor's words, while damning, only scratched the surface of the truth she sought.

"Their actions have cost innocent people millions," the prosecutor continued, her voice rising with righteous indignation.

Millions, Cartier scoffed. If only they knew the true cost – lives shattered, families torn apart. The Peachtree Syndicate's tendrils reached far deeper than mere financial fraud.

Callie's manicured nails tapped a silent rhythm on the polished wood of the defense table. Her mind whirred, constructing and discarding strategies with ruthless efficiency. The Valentine's Day gala loomed in her memory, a glittering facade concealing treachery. Who among their so-called allies had turned? And how to neutralize them?

"Mr. Cohn, are you ready to proceed?" Judge Hargrove's voice cut through any calculations.

"Always, Your Honor," Mr. Cohn replied, rising to his feet.

As he launched into his opening statement, Callie's eyes wandered to the gallery. There, nestled inconspicuously among the spectators, a face that shouldn't exist. Lila Richardson who sat perfectly still.

Beneath Lila's elegant facade, Callie's piercing gaze upon her made her uneasy. She was this close to having her plan executed flawlessly. She was calculating, assessing. Lila's fingers itched to reach for her phone, to contact Bradley.

Following the gala, Lila was convinced that the stakes had been raised exponentially. The Peachtree Syndicate's public display against Bradley was a power play, and now his position had become precarious. Lila had no intention of allowing them to destabilize everything she worked for. Perhaps it was time to sever her connection with Bradley and the Syndicate, she mused, shifting her focus to the defense's opening statement.

"Ladies and gentlemen of the jury," Mr. Cohn's voice resonated through the courtroom, "the prosecution would have you believe that my clients are nothing more than criminals masquerading as pillars of society. But I assure you, the evidence will show otherwise."

Lila's mind whirled, formulating plans even as she maintained her outward calm. How vulnerable is Bradley and how can I use it to my advantage? Did he destroy all the files as instructed? Is my lover now a liability?

"You okay?" a low voice murmured beside her. Lila turned slightly to see an elderly woman eyeing her with concern.

"Just fine, thank you," Lila replied softly, her Southern charm effortlessly masking her inner turmoil. "These proceedings can be quite intense."

As Mr. Cohn continued his opening statement, Lila's gaze locked with Cartier's for a brief, electric moment. In that instant, a wealth of unspoken history passed between them – love, betrayal, secrets long buried but never forgotten.

"The truth," Mr. Cohn declared, "is that CR Enterprises has always operated with the utmost integrity and transparency."

Lila suppressed a cynical laugh. If only they knew the depths of deception that lay beneath the polished surface of Atlanta's elite.

As the courtroom drama unfolded before her, Lila steeled herself for the battles to come. She had not come this far to falter now.

As the opening statements concluded, Lila slipped out of the courtroom, her heels clicking softly on the polished floor. As she approached the elevators she saw Serenity, Audra and Donovan talking in a secluded alcove, their faces etched with concern.

"Well?" Audra asked, her vibrant auburn hair a stark contrast to the muted tones of the courthouse.

Donovan shook his head. "They're building a solid case, but it's all surface-level." He leaned in, his voice barely above a whisper. "I may have something. An old contact from CR Enterprises reached out. Says he has information about offshore accounts."

"Can we trust him?" Serenity was now skeptical of everyone except her immediate circle.

Audra's lips curved into a mischievous smile. "Leave that to me. I have ways of verifying information."

Serenity nodded, a plan forming. "We need to move fast. The prosecution's case is strong, but if we can prove Cartier was being manipulated..."

"It's a dangerous game," Donovan warned, his eyes darting around the hallway. "The Syndicate won't take kindly to us poking around."

"True," Serenity agreed, her voice hardening with resolve. "But we're out of options. It's time to bring the shadows into the light."

Lila's sudden appearance startled the trio. "I didn't notice you all in the courtroom," she announced.

"We were seated towards the back," Donovan replied with a mocking grin.

"Serenity, I understand it must be challenging for you. Not being able to sit in the courtroom because you're the prosecutor's star witness," Lila remarked, smiling knowingly.

"Challenges come with the territory," Serenity replied cryptically. "But I must do the right thing, not only for you Lila, also for the company."

A tense stillness enveloped the group as Lila carefully observed each member, trying to discern their alliances and motives. Suddenly, her phone rang, and she excused herself to take the call from Bradley. As she walked away, the trio exchanged knowing looks, aware that Lila was up to something devious.

"You all return to the courtroom and take notes," Serenity instructed Audra and Donovan. "I have a lead to pursue. We'll reconvene later to discuss our progress." As she made her way to exit, Serenity crossed paths with Lila, exchanging forced smiles before stepping onto the elevator.

The courtroom fell into a tense hush as the prosecution called their first witness. Audra leaned forward, focusing as she recognized the man taking the stand—Marcus Holloway, a former mid-level executive at CR Enterprises.

Cartier's jaw tightened subtly, while Callie maintained her facade of cool indifference. Audra's gaze flicked between them, reading the subtle shifts in their demeanor.

"Mr. Holloway," the prosecutor began, her voice crisp and authoritative, "can you describe the events leading up to the Peachtree Project's collapse?"

Marcus cleared his throat, his fingers fidgeting with his tie. "It was chaos. Mr. Richardson and Ms. Morgan were pushing for impossible deadlines, demanding we cut corners to maximize profits."

Audra's pen moved swiftly across her notepad, dissecting his every word. Something about his testimony felt off, rehearsed.

"And did you voice your concerns?" the prosecutor pressed.

"I tried," Marcus replied, his voice wavering. "But they threatened my job, my family. Said they had powerful friends who could make us disappear."

A ripple of murmurs swept through the courtroom. Audra nudged Donovan's arm, catching the almost undetectable twitch in Marcus' left eye—a tell she remembered from staff negotiation meetings years ago.

"He's lying," Audra whispered to Donovan, "or at least not telling the whole truth."

As Marcus continued his damning testimony, Audra and Donovan both wondered, who was pulling his strings? What leverage did they have over him?

Audra glanced at Cartier, noting the tension in his shoulders, the barely contained fury in his eyes. He knew Marcus was distorting the truth, but why? What game was being played here?

Audra's pen paused over her notepad, listening intently as she observed Marcus's testimony unfold. His words painted a picture of Cartier and Callie as ruthless tyrants, but something in his demeanor didn't quite align with the narrative he was weaving.

"Mr. Richardson personally oversaw the reallocation of funds," Marcus continued, his voice steady but his hands trembling slightly. "He insisted on moving millions into offshore accounts, threatening anyone who questioned his motives."

Audra's pen glided across her notepad. She jotted down: 'Offshore accounts - trace transactions. M's body language inconsistent. Pressure from outside?'

As Marcus described a particularly damning encounter with Callie, Donovan caught a fleeting glance between the witness and someone in the gallery. It was so brief, he almost missed it. His pulse quickened as he discreetly scanned the courtroom, trying to identify the silent communicator.

"Did you catch that?" Donovan mumbled to Audra, but she was too focused on taking notes and didn't hear him.

"And Ms. Morgan, she was equally complicit?" the prosecutor prodded.

Marcus nodded, a bead of sweat forming on his brow. "She orchestrated the cover-up, manipulated the books. Her financial expertise was... unparalleled."

Audra's pen paused mid-sentence. 'Unparalleled?' The choice of word struck her as odd, almost admiring. She glanced at Callie, noting the slight tilt of her head, the ghost of a smirk playing at the corners of her mouth.

'Connection between M and C?' Audra scribbled, her mind already formulating a plan to dig deeper into their relationship. As the cross-examination began, she leaned forward, every fiber of her being attuned to the subtle dance of truth and deception playing out before her.

The defense attorney rose, his demeanor a study in controlled aggression. "Mr. Holloway, you claim to have intimate knowledge of CR Enterprises' financial dealings. Yet, your position was that of a mid-level analyst, correct?"

Marcus shifted in his seat, his confidence faltering. "I... yes, that's correct."

Audra suspected something off about Marcus' testimony but couldn't quite place it. Now, as doubt crept into his voice, her senses heightened.

"And how, Mr. Holloway, did a mid-level analyst gain access to such sensitive information?" the attorney's voice dripped with skepticism.

Marcus fumbled with his tie. "I... I overheard conversations. Saw documents I wasn't meant to see."

A low murmur rippled through the courtroom. Audra caught Donovan's eye, a silent communication passing between them. Audra nodded, already jotting down notes.

The attorney pounced. "Overheard conversations? Saw documents? Mr. Holloway, are you asking this court to believe that you stumbled upon evidence of a massive financial conspiracy through happenstance?"

Marcus' composure crumbled. "No, I... There were meetings, late at night. I stayed late, I heard things."

Donovan shook his head. Late-night meetings? That didn't align with Cartier's meticulously scheduled routine or Callie's. He glanced at them, noting the slight furrow in their brows. They were thinking the same thing.

As the cross-examination continued, the atmosphere in the courtroom shifted palpably. Jurors exchanged glances, their earlier certainty giving way to confusion. While the defense attorney continued to pick apart Marcus Holloway's testimony, Audra's fingers moved swiftly across her phone's screen. Her message to Serenity: "Holloway's cracking. Late-night meetings don't add up. Digging deeper."

At some point, Mr. Cohn came across a message that Cartier had hastily jotted down on a scrap of paper, causing him to pause. "Your Honor, I move for a brief recess," Cartier's attorney announced, his voice cutting through Audra's thoughts.

The judge nodded, "Very well. Court will recess for fifteen minutes."

The moment the courtroom began to clear out for recess, Audra and Donovan quickly made their way to a quiet area, as there was a lot to discuss and analyze from the proceedings so far.

The courthouse steps buzzed with reporters, microphones thrust forward like weapons, but Serenity Richardson moved through the chaos with an air of steely determination. Cartier and Morgan's trial was in full swing, and while the circus inside the courtroom played out, Serenity had bigger priorities. A lead from an unexpected source hinted at evidence that could bring Lila and Bradley's web of deceit crashing down. Serenity wasn't going to miss the chance to follow it.

Clad in a sleek navy trench coat and heels that clicked sharply against the pavement, she wove through the throng of onlookers. Her target was an informant waiting two blocks away—a former associate of Bradley's who had promised a critical piece of the puzzle. Her pace quickened as she moved farther from the courthouse. The sounds of the city engulfed her, the honking cars and distant chatter a far cry from the tension of the courthouse.

The meeting location was a secluded alleyway. It wasn't ideal, but they were pressed for time. She adjusted her navy trench coat, her keen eyes scanning the area as she approached. She spotted a man anxiously pacing back and forth, waiting for her arrival.

Serenity remained calm but guarded as she got closer to the individual standing before her. The man, mid-30s with a wiry frame, stepped closer. His hood obscured most of his face, but his unease was unmistakable. "Serenity Richardson?" he asked in a low tone.

"That's right," she replied. "Do you have what I need?"

The man glanced around the alley; his paranoia evident. "Yeah. I have it," he said, pulling a small flash drive from his jacket pocket. "But I don't think we were as careful as we thought. We've got company."

Before Serenity could respond, she heard the faint scuff of shoes on concrete. Her stomach tightened as she turned her head slightly, catching movement from the corner of her eye. Figures emerged from the shadows, their intent clear in the predatory way they moved.

The man froze, his eyes wide with fear. "They're here for us," he whispered hoarsely, shoving the flash drive into her hand. "Take it. Get out of here!"

Before she could react, one of the attackers lunged at her with a sharp knife. Serenity swiftly sidestepped the attack, her heel striking the attacker's knee with force. He stumbled and dropped the blade, momentarily stunned.

"Run!" The informant yelled to Serenity. They both pivoted to flee, but another assailant charged at the informant from behind. The informant dodged just in time and landed a powerful punch to the attacker's stomach before scrambling towards the alleyway exit.

A burly man lunged at Serenity, forcing her to dodge backward. Her back hit the brick wall, but she reacted swiftly, using her momentum to deliver a sharp elbow to his ribs. He grunted in pain, but his grip on her wrist was unyielding.

"You don't know when to quit, do you?" the man growled, tightening his hold.

Serenity twisted her body, delivering a powerful knee strike to his stomach, causing him to release her with a painful wheeze. Without hesitation, she grabbed a discarded metal pipe nearby, landing a solid blow to his jaw. Clutching the flash drive, she secured it in her purse before bolting toward the end of the alley. Her heels slowed her down, so she kicked them off mid-run, the cold pavement biting at her feet.

The man pursued her, his heavy footsteps closing the gap. Serenity spotted a stack of crates near a fire escape. With a burst of energy, she jumped onto the crates and grabbed the ladder, pulling herself up just as the man reached for her ankle. His fingers brushed her skin, but she climbed higher, fueled by desperation.

Reaching the rooftop, Serenity paused to catch her breath. Below, the assailant cursed loudly, realizing he couldn't follow. She crouched low, heart hammering in her chest.

Serenity allowed herself a moment of relief before the gravity of the situation set in. At this point, she wasn't sure if it was Lila and Bradley who were playing a dangerous game, or the Peachtree Syndicate. Regardless, it was clear someone was willing to go to any lengths to silence her.

Chapter Twelve

The Fire Beneath

The night air was thick with the scent of rain, though the storm had yet to break. Serenity sat in the faintly lit corner of a nondescript safe house; the flash drive clenched tightly in her hand. The room smelled slightly of mildew, its single lamp casting long shadows on the peeling wallpaper. Across from her, the informant—whose name she had learned was Wesley—paced nervously, glancing at the boarded-up window as though expecting an army to storm through it at any moment.

"They'll come after you harder now," Wesley muttered, his voice shaky. "You've got something they can't afford to let out."

Serenity placed the drive on the small table between them and leaned forward, her piercing gaze locking on him. "Then I need to know exactly what's on this. I need details, Wesley. Who sent you? Why now?"

He ran a hand through his hair, sighing heavily. "I worked for Bradley. Not directly—more like one of his errand boys. Cleaning up messes, tying up loose ends. Until I found out I was the loose end." His eyes darted toward the door. "That's when I started collecting insurance."

Serenity's eyes narrowed. "Insurance?"

"Files. Transactions. Recordings. Proof of what Lila and Bradley have been up to. Blackmail, bribery, murder—it's all there." He gestured toward the drive, his expression grim. "That thing. It's your smoking gun. But it's also a target painted on your back."

Serenity was aware of the danger beforehand, so his warning didn't make her flinch. "Why now, Wesley? Why risk coming forward?"

His pacing stopped, and he turned to face her, his face pale but resolute. "Because they killed my brother. He worked for CR Enterprises;

thought he was untouchable. Until he stumbled onto one of their 'special projects.' I tried to warn him to stay quiet, but..." His voice broke, and he looked away. "I couldn't save him. But maybe this can bring them down."

Serenity exhaled slowly, her grip on the edge of the table tightening. "I'm sorry for your loss. But if this is as big as you say it is, we need to move fast. Bradley and Lila will stop at nothing to bury this—and us."

Wesley nodded. "I know a guy. A tech wizard. He can extract everything on that drive, verify it, and help you use it without getting caught."

Serenity raised an eyebrow. "Can we trust him?" that had become her go-to question.

"I trust him more than anyone else right now," Wesley said. "But we'll have to be careful. They're watching everything."

Before Serenity could respond, the sound of hurried footsteps approached the door. Instinctively, her hand went to the pipe she had kept close since the alley attack. Wesley froze, his eyes wide.

The knock came next, sharp and deliberate. Serenity's pulse quickened as she edged closer to the door. "Who is it?" she called, her voice firm.

"It's us!" a familiar voice answered. "Audra

and Donovan. Serenity, open up! We got your text. Are you okay?"

Relief washed over her, but it was fleeting. She cracked the door open just enough to see Audra's worried face and Donovan standing protectively behind her, scanning the area. Serenity stepped aside to let them in.

Audra, dressed in a raincoat with her auburn curls damp from the drizzle, immediately grabbed Serenity's shoulders, her eyes searching her face. "What happened? Are you hurt?"

"I'm fine," Serenity assured her, though her voice carried a weight that spoke of the day's events."

Donovan, tall and broad-shouldered, closed the door firmly behind him, locking it before turning his sharp gaze on Wesley. "And who's this?" his tone wasn't hostile, but there was a clear edge of protectiveness.

"This is Wesley," Serenity said, gesturing toward the informant. "He's the one who got us this." She held up the flash drive. "It's everything we need to take Lila and Bradley down."

Donovan folded his arms, assessing Wesley with a skeptical look. "You sure we can trust him?"

"Yes," Serenity said firmly. "He's risked his

life to get this to me. And he's already lost someone because of Lila and Bradley."

Wesley nodded, his expression earnest. "I'm not here to cause trouble. I just want to make sure they don't get away with what they've done."

A crack of thunder echoed outside, and Serenity's gaze flicked toward the window. The storm was finally here. "Where is this tech wizard you trust?" she turned to Wesley and asked.

"An old workshop on the outskirts of town. It's off the grid. No cameras, no prying eyes."

Serenity stood, slipping the flash drive into her purse. "Then let's go."

Audra's eyes softened slightly, turning to Serenity. "We're coming with you. You shouldn't be out there alone, especially now."

Serenity hesitated for a moment, but Donovan interjected before she could protest. "Don't argue, Serenity. We're a team on this, and you know it. Whatever's coming, we face it together."

A faint smile tugged at Serenity's lips. She had known Audra and Donovan long enough to understand that they wouldn't take no for an answer. "All right," she said. "But we have to move fast. Wesley's contact is off the grid, and we can't stay here."

Audra nodded. "Then let's go. Oh," she paused briefly, reaching into her duffel bag. "I brought the shoes you asked for."

"I can't go anywhere without shoes—thank you!" Serenity said, slipping them on without hesitation.

As they stepped out into the night, the rain began to fall, soaking the cracked pavement and masking their footsteps. Serenity's instincts were on high alert, every shadow a potential threat. This was no longer just about survival. It was about justice. And she would stop at nothing to see it served.

The fire beneath her was burning brighter now, fueled by every lie, every betrayal, and every life Lila and Bradley had destroyed. Serenity wasn't just playing defense anymore—she was preparing to strike. And when she did, she wouldn't miss.

The rain poured down in a relentless deluge, drenching the small group as they got in the car and made their way through the darkened streets. Wesley drove with purpose and determination.

As they approached the outskirts of town, the workshop came into view—a dilapidated structure nestled among overgrown weeds and abandoned machinery. The only light emanated from a small window on the second floor, casting a dim glow on the rain-slicked ground.

Wesley scanned their surroundings warily, his senses hyper-aware when they pulled up. "We need to be cautious. There's no telling if we're being followed."

Serenity nodded, her focus sharp as she surveyed the area. The oppressive darkness and the pelting rain added to the sense of urgency that hung in the air. She could feel the weight of the mission pressing down on her, the gravity of what was at stake.

Donovan stepped out first, his tall frame cutting a confident silhouette in the darkness. "We stick together," Donovan said, his voice low but firm. "Watch each other's backs."

Audra reached for Serenity's hand, a silent gesture of solidarity and support. "We've come this far. We won't let anything stop us now."

They made their way to the workshop entrance, the creaking of the rusty door echoed in the stillness of the night. Inside, the air was musty and thick with the scent of old metal and sweat.

The workshop was a maze of shadows and forgotten relics, machinery draped in dusty cloths, and shelves lined with tools long untouched. A lone figure stood at a cluttered workbench, surrounded by computer parts and wires.

The tech wizard turned around, revealing a young man with bright blue eyes and a messy shock of blond hair. His gaze flashed from Wesley to the rest of the group, curiosity and caution in his expression.

"You weren't followed, were you?" the tech wizard questioned, his voice filled nervous intensity.

Wesley shook his head. "We took precautions, but we can't waste any time."

Serenity stepped forward. "You're the one who can decrypt the drive and verify its contents?"

The tech wizard nodded. "That's me. They call me Cipher." He gestured to the mess of equipment around him. "I've got everything we need right here to crack this baby open."

Donovan stood next to Serenity; his stare shrewd as he examined the setup. "How long will it take?"

Cipher shrugged, "Depends on how well they've encrypted it. Could be minutes, could be hours. But I'm one of the best in the business."

The tech wizard's eyes widened as Serenity handed him the flash drive. With nimble fingers, he inserted it into a laptop and began the decryption process. Lines of code scrolled rapidly across the screen; his forehead wrinkling from deep concentration. After a few tense moments, the tech wizard's eyes widened slightly.

"This is some seriously sophisticated encryption," Cipher uttered, his fingers flying over the keyboard. "They really didn't want anyone getting their hands on this."

Serenity watched intently, her heart pounding with a combination of anticipation and dread. Each passing second felt like an eternity, the only sound in the room the soft hum of the equipment and the patter of rain against the window.

Finally, with a soft beep, the screen displayed a list of files that had been successfully decrypted. Serenity leaned in closer, scanning the contents. There it was the incriminating evidence that could unravel Lila and Bradley's web of deceit. Each file was a piece of the puzzle, revealing the depths of corruption within CR Enterprises.

"We got them," Serenity announced with a fierce determination.

Chapter Thirteen

Double-Cross

The soft rhythm of Serenity's heels striking the polished marble reverberated through the silent corridors of CR Enterprises. Each deliberate step carried her closer to Bradley's office, a fortress of influence perched high above Atlanta's glittering skyline. Beneath the poised façade she wore so impeccably, her mind held a storm of strategies and contingencies.

Serenity paused before the imposing door, drawing a measured breath. She mimicked the mask of Lila—confident, enigmatic, unassailable—settled over her features like a second skin. With a gentle push, she entered.

Bradley Upton's piercing gaze met hers instantly. He rose, his tall frame cutting an impressive silhouette against the floor-to-ceiling windows behind him.

"Ms. Clayborn," he intoned, gesturing to the chair across from his desk. "Please, have a seat."

Serenity glided forward, her movements fluid and purposeful. As she lowered herself into the plush leather chair, she cataloged every minute detail of Bradley's demeanor—the slight tension in his jaw, the way his fingers drummed once against his thigh before sitting.

'He's on edge,' she mused.' Good. Let him wonder what I know.'

"Thank you for meeting with me on such short notice, Serenity," Bradley said, his voice a carefully modulated blend of warmth and professionalism.

"Of course," Serenity nodded, settling into her chair. "How are you feeling? We haven't had a chance to speak since your altercation at the gala."

"I'm fine. Thank you for asking. I've moved on from that unfortunate incident," Bradley said, smoothly shifting the conversation, signaling he had no desire to discuss it any further. "I've been meaning to speak with you privately."

"What's on your mind?" Serenity allowed the barest hint of a smile to play across her lips, a calculated show of confidence.

"We have a shared past, collaborating alongside Cynthia. Sadly, she is no longer with us. Your efforts at CR Enterprises have not gone unnoticed. You are responsible for exposing the corruption and holding Cartier and Callie accountable for their actions, including Cynthia's murder."

"The trial is still ongoing, so we shall see if justice prevails, but thank you, I'm flattered," she replied. "Though I can't help but wonder about the true nature of this meeting. Surely, you didn't call me here simply to offer praise."

"Direct, aren't you? I appreciate that in a colleague."

"In my experience," she countered smoothly, "directness can be a valuable asset in our line of work. Particularly when the stakes are high."

A ghost of a smile touched Bradley's lips. "Indeed. And the stakes at CR Enterprises are always high, wouldn't you agree?"

Serenity leaned forward slightly, her gaze locked in. "Absolutely. Which is why I'm most curious to hear what you have in mind, Bradley. I suspect this conversation will prove... illuminating for us both."

The tension in the room ratcheted up another notch, a silent battle of wills unfolding in the space between them. Serenity was analyzing every nuance of Bradley's body language, every carefully chosen word. Whatever his true motives, she knew one thing with certainty: this meeting would mark a turning point in her mission.

Bradley reclined back in his chair, fingers steepled beneath his chin. "Let's talk about Lila," he said, his tone deceptively casual.

"What about Lila?" she asked, her tone carefully even, laced with a touch of curiosity.

Bradley's lips curled into a faint, calculating smile. "Remove Lila from her throne," he proposed, with a polished ease. "I've been observing her leadership closely," he continued, his gaze never leaving Serenity's face. "And I've come to a rather... unsettling conclusion."

"What might that be?" Serenity inquired, tactfully crossing her legs and shifting in her seat.

"Lila's recklessness has begun to strain our most valuable partnerships. I can't get into details, but she is responsible for the discord with Peachtree Syndicate, and I've been left to clean up her mess. I fear Lila's ambition may be leading us down a dangerous path. If we don't act soon, CR Enterprises may not recover. So, for the good of the company I believe it's time for a change in leadership. And I want your help to make it happen."

Bradley was playing a dangerous game, and now he was trying to pull Serenity into it. "And by 'we,' you mean me?" she asked, feigning ignorance. "Why would I have any part in this?"

"Because," Bradley said, his voice soft yet sharp, "you stand to gain as much as I do. Lila's downfall would leave a power vacuum. With your expertise and influence, you could easily step into a more prominent role—if not at the top, then very close to it. You've proven your loyalty to this company, Serenity. I'd rather see it in capable hands like yours than watch it crumble under hers."

Serenity crossed her arms, her eyes narrowing as she studied him. "You're asking me to betray her. To help you orchestrate a coup."

"I'm asking you to do what's necessary," Bradley countered, his tone growing firmer. "This isn't personal—it's business. And if you're smart, you'll realize this is an opportunity, not a betrayal."

Opportunity, Serenity thought, considering Bradley's offer. Accepting it meant walking a tightrope with one of the most cunning players in the game.

"I'll need to think about this." Serenity rose to leave, but paused, glancing back at Bradley with a deliberate look on her face. "One last thing," she said, her voice light yet edged with curiosity.

Bradley leaned back in his chair again. "Go on."

"Are you aware that Lila and Callie knew each other as teenagers?" Serenity casually asked.

Bradley's composure faltered for the briefest of moments. "I wasn't," he admitted, his tone carefully neutral. "Are you sure?"

Serenity's expression was unreadable. "Positive. I stumbled upon the information while delving into the company's history. It struck me as... intriguing."

Bradley's gaze sharpened, but before he could press further, Serenity continued. "Anyway, something to think about. I'll be in touch."

With that, she turned and exited his office, her steps intentional as her mind cataloged his reaction. She hadn't missed the flicker of surprise in his eyes—or the guarded look that followed. *That rattled him*, she thought. *Good.*

The pieces on the board were shifting, and Serenity was ready to make her next move.

The soft ticking of the Cartier clock on her desk echoed like a taunt in Lila Richardson's opulent office. Her fingers drummed an impatient rhythm against the glass, each tap a reflection of her restless thoughts.

"They're closing in," she muttered, her voice barely above a whisper. "I can feel it."

Lila's gaze darted to the security monitors discretely embedded in her desk, scanning for any sign of threat. The familiar corridors of CR Enterprises appeared calm, but appearances could be deceiving. She knew better than anyone how easily a facade of tranquility could mask treachery.

Rising abruptly, Lila strode to the wet bar. She poured herself two fingers of aged scotch, the amber liquid a poor balm for her frayed nerves.

"I won't let them take what's mine," she vowed, her reflection in the mirror behind the bar betraying a flash of willpower in her eyes. "It's time to make my move."

As she sipped her drink, Lila pondered who remained loyal to her and who might be her enemies. She'd be damned if she'd let anyone wrest power from her grasp.

"Bradley," she murmured, setting down her glass with newfound resolve. "He'll be the key."

Serenity leaned over her laptop, fingers dancing across the keyboard as she navigated a maze of decrypted files that Cipher shared with her. She was searching for the final piece to drive the nail into Lila's coffin.

"Come on, come on," she huffed, her heart hammering a rapid rhythm against her chest. "Where are you hiding?"

Serenity's phone let out a faint notification sound, startling her. She glanced down at the message, a reminder of the looming court date where she was scheduled to testify for the prosecution at Cartier's trial. The heaviness of her responsibility crashed down on her once more, almost drowning her with its overwhelming force. But she was determined to have every detail in place before she testified, like a perfectly aligned puzzle.

"I won't let you down, Cartier," she vowed, returning to her digital excavation with renewed vigor. "Not this time."

As another file yielded its secrets, Serenity's breath caught in her throat. Hidden among the mundane spreadsheets and memos, there it was, one last piece that would be the final blow – a bow to tie around the package that would destroy Lila's world. Now, all Serenity needed to know was who murdered Cynthia.

Chapter Fourteen

The Mastermind's Gambit

Serenity slipped into the back of the room, just as Lila swept in, her silk blouse rustling softly with each purposeful stride. She took her place at the head of the table, her glare lingering on Bradley Upton's impassive face. The executives of CR Enterprises sat upright; their expressions carefully composed.

Lila's voice cut through the silence. "Ladies and gentlemen, I've called this meeting to discuss the future of our company. A future that requires... decisive action. We're at a crossroads. Our competitors are circling like vultures, and we must act decisively."

Bradley leaned forward; his brow furrowed. "What exactly are you proposing, Lila?"

"Our current structure leaves us vulnerable to outside influences," Lila paused her gaze sweeping the room. "I propose a complete reorganization that will consolidate power and streamline decision-making."

A murmur rippled through the room. Serenity caught Bradley's eye, seeing her own concern mirrored in his face. This was daring, even for Lila.

"Mrs. Richardson," one of the older board members spoke up, his voice quavering slightly, "such a drastic change could destabilize—"

"Destabilize?" Lila interrupted, her smile not quite reaching her eyes. "Or revolutionize? Change is the lifeblood of business. We adapt, or we die."

"This is a bold move, Lila," Bradley interjected, his tone measured but his eyes betraying a flicker of concern. "This is a drastic shift in power dynamics."

Lila's eyes glinted with determination. "It's a necessary shift. You all will be pleased once you see the results. We're not just reshuffling; we're fortifying our position against any... internal threats."

With a predator's grin, Lila outlined her plan, the atmosphere in the room grew increasingly tense. Some nodded in agreement, while others exchanged worried glances. Lila's words painted a future of unchecked power, thinly veiled as corporate efficiency

As the board meeting adjourned, the tension in the room was palpable. Serenity watched as executives huddled in small groups, their hushed whispers carrying traces of fear and uncertainty.

"Did you see Frank's face?" a junior executive muttered to his colleague. "I've never seen him so pale."

"This reorganization... it's going to shake things up," the colleague replied, his voice tinged with anxiety.

Serenity was gathering her notes when she felt a firm grip on her arm. Lila greeted her with one of her perfectly practiced smiles.

"Serenity," Lila said smoothly, her voice low but commanding. "Do you have a moment?"

Serenity paused, her face a portrait of professionalism. "Of course, Lila. What's on your mind?"

Lila gestured toward a quiet corner of the sleek conference room. As they stepped away from the exiting executives, she leaned in, her tone dripping with forced kindheartedness. "I've noticed some... tension between us lately. I hope I haven't done anything to make you feel undervalued."

Serenity tilted her head slightly, meeting Lila's gaze with a polite smile. "Not at all. If anything, I've been even more focused on ensuring CR Enterprises remains on course with you leading the way."

"Good," Lila said, her smile shifting to one of optimism. "Because staying aligned is crucial—especially with everything happening right now." She glanced around, ensuring no one was in earshot, before continuing. "Cartier's trial is a critical moment for all of us. The company's reputation hangs in the balance, and we both know how important it is that he and Callie are held accountable for their actions."

Serenity's stomach churned at the blatant manipulation, but she didn't let it show. "Naturally," she agreed.

Lila's expression softened, though her calculating nature remained evident. "I need to know that when you testify, you'll be clear about their involvement. It's imperative that the jury sees the truth."

Serenity locked eyes with Lila, her voice honey sweet and convincing. "You don't need to worry about me, Lila. When I take the stand, I'll make sure there's no doubt about Cartier and Callie's culpability. Remember, I always have your back."

"I knew I could count on you, Serenity. You've always been loyal to me, ever since we were little girls growing up in foster care together. I appreciate that more than you know." Lila radiated self-satisfaction.

"You know my loyalty has always been to you, and that hasn't changed," Serenity said, gripping Lila's arm doing her own subtle cunning. "But I'm still expecting that promotion and raise once you close the Langston deal," she added with a playful wink, "

"Of course. It's well deserved," Lila said, patting Serenity's arm lightly as if she was her dutiful lap dog. "But before we start celebrating. Your promotion and pay raise, let's make sure this chapter ends with the right people paying for their mistakes. Cartier is a monster, and you must make sure the jury sees that."

"I promise. I will tell the jury exactly what

they need to hear. We will get justice, Lila." she vowed.

Serenity moved through the corridors of CR Enterprises, observing the ripple effects of Lila's announcement. Alliances were shifting before her eyes, loyalties tested in the crucible of corporate ambition.

"We need to talk," Donovan whispered as he passed her, his eyes darting nervously. "My office, ten minutes."

Serenity nodded, right as her phone vibrated. A message from an unknown number:

The truth lies in the shadows of the Peach. Meet me at midnight if you want to save everything.

As she stared at the cryptic message, Serenity wondered if Lila was setting a trap. She had to find out either way.

The city was cloaked in a restless silence as Serenity made her way to the meeting place—a derelict industrial lot on the outskirts of Atlanta, nicknamed "The Peach" for its proximity to a now-defunct peach cannery. The air was thick with the scent of damp asphalt, and the dim light of a flickering streetlamp cast eerie shadows across the cracked pavement.

Serenity pulled her coat tighter around her shoulders, her pulse steady but her mind racing. The cryptic message had left her uneasy, but curiosity and the promise of answers propelled her forward. Her hand lingered near the small canister of pepper spray in her pocket as she scanned the area.

A figure emerged from the shadows, their silhouette tall and lean. They stepped into the weak glow of the streetlamp, revealing a man in his late forties with tired eyes and a wary expression. His dark jacket hung loosely on his strapping frame. His hands were raised slightly to show he meant no harm.

"Serenity," the man called out. "I wasn't sure you'd come."

"Who are you?" she asked, her stance guarded. "And how do you know about me?"

"My name's Victor," he replied, taking a cautious step closer. "I used to work for Cartier Richardson, back when CR Enterprises was just starting to rise. And I know things—things about Lila and Callie that you need to hear."

Serenity's eyes narrowed. "This better not be a waste of my time."

"It won't be," Victor assured her. "But we don't have long. If Lila finds out I'm talking to you, we're both as good as dead."

"Start talking," Serenity said, her voice edged with impatience.

Victor glanced over his shoulder before continuing. "Not sure if you're aware of this but Lila and Callie go way back—teenagers. Lila was in the foster care system, but they developed a friendship."

"I was in foster care with Lila. However, I only recently became aware that she and Callie have history, Lila kept that a secret from me."

"For good reason. From my understanding, Lila and Callie were both very ambitious and conniving. Together, they became better master manipulators. At some point they drifted apart, but years later, after Lila married Cartier, she ran into Callie again. Lila saw an opportunity."

Serenity folded her arms, her sharp gaze fixed on Victor. "What kind of opportunity?"

Victor hesitated, then took a deep breath. "Cartier was a serial cheater. Lila knew it. She was tired of being the long-suffering wife and wanted to teach him a lesson while securing her place in the company. She convinced Callie to seduce Cartier, to bait him into an affair that Lila could use as leverage. It was all part of her plan to take control of CR Enterprises."

Serenity nodded, intrigued by what she was learning. "Clearly something went wrong. Callie is currently behind bars. On trial facing a plethora of charges, while Lila sits comfortably on the throne."

"Very wrong," Victor confirmed. "Callie didn't just play her part—she fell for Cartier. And worse, for a brief period of time, Cartier fell for her too. However, while Callie remained deeply in love him, as was typical for Cartier, his romantic feelings for Callie fizzled out. Despite this, she refused to give up on their relationship. That wasn't part of Lila's plan. She felt betrayed—by both of them."

Serenity's stomach clenched into a knot. "So, Lila turned on them."

Victor nodded grimly. "She decided to take everything from Cartier and make Callie pay for her betrayal. She faked her own death, planting evidence to make it look like Cartier and Callie were involved in Cynthia's murder. Then she fabricated the corporate crimes, using her inside knowledge to frame them both. Lila didn't just want revenge—she wanted complete annihilation."

"And you know all of this because…"

"Because I helped her," Victor admitted, his voice tinged with regret. "At first, I thought it was just business. I didn't know the full extent of her plans until it was too late. By the time I realized what she was doing, I was in too deep."

"Why come forward now?" Serenity asked, her tone cutting.

Victor's shoulders sagged. "Because I'm tired of being another one of Lila's puppets. And because people like Lila don't stop until everyone who knows the truth is silenced. You're her biggest threat now, and the only person that is probably capable of taking her down."

"Do you have proof?" Serenity demanded.

Victor nodded, handing the large envelope he was holding. "It's all here—emails, recordings, financial transactions and the murder weapon. Everything you need to expose her."

Serenity couldn't contain her curiosity any longer. "I know Bradley Upton is working with Lila. Did he also kill Cynthia? she had to know the truth. "

"No."

"Was it you?" she pressed.

Victor shook his head. "Lila committed the deed herself, but she asked me to dispose of the weapon," he revealed. "I kept it as insurance. Be cautious, Serenity. Lila's always thinking ahead and planning her next move. Don't be another casualty in grand scheme," he warned.

As Victor faded back into the shadows, Serenity stared down at the envelope in her hand, her grip tightening. All of the truth had finally come to light, but the fight was far from over. If Lila wanted a war, Serenity was ready to give her one.

Chapter Fifteen

Courtroom Showdown

The heavy oak doors of the courtroom creaked open, and Serenity Clayborn stepped through, her presence commanding the room like a force of nature. The soft hum of murmurs that had filled the air moments earlier evaporated, replaced by an oppressive silence as every eye turned to her.

She wore a fitted charcoal-gray suit that exuded authority and elegance, its sharp lines softened by a silk blouse in a deep emerald hue. A pair of black stilettos clicked against the polished marble floor as she strode toward the witness stand, her every step measured, deliberate. Her hair, swept back into a sleek bun, revealed the striking angles of her face, and the faintest glint of gold earrings caught the light as she moved. Her expression was unreadable.

The courtroom was packed, the weight of the trial palpable in the air. On one side, Cartier Richardson sat at the defense table, his gaze locked on Serenity with an intensity that seemed to burn. Beside him, Callie, who appeared more defiant than ever. On the other side, the prosecution team watched Serenity like hawks, high expectations looming.

As she reached the witness stand, the bailiff stepped forward, motioning for her to raise her right hand. "Do you swear to tell the truth, the whole truth, and nothing but the truth, so help you God?"

"I do," Serenity said, her voice steady, reverberating in the silent room.

She took her seat, smoothing her skirt and matching jacket as she settled in.

The prosecutor paced slowly in front of the witness stand, his own tailored suit pristine and his tone deliberate. Serenity sat poised, her hands folded neatly in her lap, the epitome of a composed professional. The courtroom hung on every word; the air thick with anticipation.

"Ms. Clayborn," the prosecutor began, stopping to face her directly, "as an executive at CR Enterprises, you had access to internal records, communications, and operational reports. Is that correct?"

"Yes," Serenity replied, her voice steady and clear.

"And during your tenure, did you observe any irregularities or concerning behaviors from Mr. Cartier Richardson or Ms. Callie Morgan?"

Serenity paused, her eyes flicking briefly toward the gallery where Lila sat in the front row, her lips curved in a faint, satisfied smile. Their eyes met, and Lila gave the subtlest nod of approval, as if to remind her childhood friend of the role she was expected to play.

"Yes," Serenity said finally. "There were incidents that raised concerns."

The prosecutor's expression tightened, his confidence growing. "Could you elaborate on those incidents for the court?"

Serenity hesitated, allowing the tension to build before speaking. "There were instances where decisions were made that seemed… questionable. Actions that could have been construed as self-serving or even unethical."

The gallery murmured, and Lila's smile widened. The prosecutor pressed on; his tone sharpened by her response. "And in your professional opinion, Ms. Clayborn, would you say these actions align with the charges against Mr. Richardson and Ms. Langston?"

"They could," Serenity replied carefully, her gaze unwavering. Lila's satisfaction was noticeable now, her posture radiating confidence as she leaned back slightly in her seat.

The prosecutor nodded, pacing again. "So, just to clarify, you believe that Mr. Richardson and Ms. Morgan acted in ways that were not only unethical but potentially criminal?"

Serenity let the question hang in the air. She glanced at Lila again, who was now sitting upright, her enthusiastic expression practically daring Serenity to continue. Then, with the faintest smile, Serenity straightened in her chair, her tone shifting to one of quiet authority.

"No," she said firmly.

The courtroom erupted in gasps and whispers. The prosecutor froze mid-step, spinning back to face her. "Excuse me, Ms. Clayborn?" he asked, his voice taut with disbelief.

"I said no," Serenity repeated, her voice louder now, cutting through the murmurs. "I do not believe Cartier Richardson and Callie Morgan are guilty of the crimes they've been charged with."

The judge banged her gavel, calling for order, but the murmurs only grew louder. Lila's confident smirk dissolved, her eyes tightening in shock. Across the courtroom, Cartier sat forward in his chair, his expression full of cautious hope. Callie's hands flew to her mouth, her wide eyes brimming with disbelief.

The prosecutor stammered, "Ms. Clayborn, can you explain why you're contradicting your earlier testimony?"

Serenity locked eyes with him, her gaze sharp as a blade. "Because I've seen evidence that points to an orchestrated effort to frame Mr. Richardson and Ms. Morgan. An effort spearheaded by Lila Richardson and her accomplice, Bradley Upton."

The courtroom exploded into chaos. Reporters whispered furiously to one another, spectators craned their necks, and even the jury appeared rattled. The judge's gavel pounded repeatedly, her voice booming, "Order! Order in this courtroom!"

The prosecutor stepped closer, his voice rising with urgency. "Ms. Clayborn, are you suggesting that Mrs. Richardson—your employer—conspired to frame her husband and Ms. Morgan?"

"Yes," Serenity said without hesitation. She turned to the jury, her voice unwavering. "I have documents, recordings, eyewitness accounts and the weapon used to murder Cynthia Johnson, that prove Lila Richardson meticulously planned her own disappearance, fabricated evidence, and manipulated this entire situation to destroy Cartier Richardson, take control of CR Enterprises, and punish Callie Morgan for betraying her."

Lila's composure cracked as she stood abruptly, color draining from her face. "This is outrageous!" She shouted, her voice shrill. "She's lying!"

The judge's gavel struck the bench. "Mrs. Richardson, sit down or you will be held in contempt!"

Serenity ignored Lila's outburst; her attention fixed on the jury. "This trial isn't about justice—it's about revenge. Cartier Richardson and Callie Morgan are victims of a calculated, ruthless scheme. And I can prove it."

The courtroom was in complete disarray, the buzz of shock and disbelief drowning out even the judge's demands for order.

Serenity relaxed in her chair, savoring the chaos she had just created.

Lila's carefully constructed empire was starting to crumble, and Serenity had just dealt the first devastating blow.

As the chaos in the courtroom swirled around her, Serenity sat unmoved, radiating unshakable confidence. She soaked in the rush of adrenaline, relishing the thrill and satisfaction of watching Lila's carefully constructed image begin to unravel. The once confident and poised Lila appeared unnerved, her facade of elegance crumbling under the weight of Serenity's accusations.

The judge's voice finally cut through the tumult, her command for order resonating with authority. The courtroom gradually quieted down, all eyes fixed on Serenity as she sat there, demure yet unyielding.

The prosecutor, still reeling from Serenity's revelation, attempted to regain control of the situation.

"Ms. Clayborn, do you have this evidence with you now?" he asked, his voice a mixture of incredulity and urgency.

Serenity nodded, a glint of determination in her eyes. "I do," she replied evenly. "And I am prepared to present it to the court."

"Your Honor, I request a brief recess to review this new evidence," the prosecutor said, his voice strained.

The gavel struck the bench sharply, the judge's voice cutting through the clamor of the courtroom. "Court will reconvene in one hour. Ms. Clayborn, you are to submit any evidence you have to the prosecutor."

Lila shot Serenity a look filled with venomous fury. Her fingers clenched into fists at her sides, a storm of emotions brewing behind her mask of composure. Cartier's gaze flitted between Serenity and Lila, realization dawning in his eyes as he processed the implications of Serenity's testimony. Beside him, Callie's stunned expression slowly morphed into a calculating glare, her mind racing to assess the damage Serenity did to the prosecution's case.

The Bailiff began to clear the gallery. The tension was profound, the mood heavy with disbelief and outrage following Serenity's bombshell testimony. Serenity stepped down from the witness stand, her heels clicking against the polished floor as she moved toward the gallery. Her head was held high, her expression calm, despite the whirlwind she had just unleashed.

As she approached the gallery, the buzz of

murmurs swelled around her. Lila Richardson, seated in the front row, was a vision of barely contained fury. Her once-pristine composure had been shattered, her eyes wild and locked onto Serenity with a venomous intensity.

Serenity didn't notice the subtle shift in the room as the bailiff moved to escort Lila out. Nor did she see Lila's sharp, sudden motion—her hand darting out, swift as a striking snake, to grab the gun from the holster at the bailiff's side.

The next moments unfolded in a blur.

"Lila, no!" someone shouted, their voice a desperate plea.

The crack of the gunshot echoed through the courtroom like thunder, freezing everyone in place. Serenity staggered, a sharp pain ripping through her side. The force of the bullet sent her collapsing to the ground, clutching her abdomen as blood began to seep through her fingers.

Screams erupted from the gallery, the once-orderly courtroom descending into chaos. Spectators scrambled for the exits, chairs toppled, and a rush of bodies surged toward safety. The bailiff tackled Lila to the ground, wrestling the weapon from her grasp as she screamed incoherently, her voice full of rage and hysteria.

"She's a liar!" Lila shrieked, her words piercing through the chaos. "She's trying to ruin everything! She deserved it!"

Cartier sprang to his feet, his face a mask of shock. "Lila, you are out of your mind!" he roared, restrained by another bailiff as he tried to move toward Serenity.

Meanwhile, Audra and Donovan both knelt beside Serenity. Donovan pressed his hands against the wound. "Stay with me, Serenity," he pleaded, his voice breaking. "Help is coming. Just hold on."

Serenity's vision blurred, her breaths shallow, but her grip on Audra's arm was firm. "This... isn't over," she whispered, her voice weak but resolute. "She won't win."

The courtroom doors burst open as paramedics rushed in, weaving through the panicked crowd. They worked quickly to stabilize Serenity, lifting her onto a stretcher as Audra and Donovan reluctantly stepped aside, tears streaming down their faces.

The judge, visibly shaken, pounded her gavel once more. "This court is adjourned until further notice. Bailiffs, detain Mrs. Richardson immediately!"

Lila was dragged from the courtroom, still thrashing against her captors, her face contorted with fury. "You'll regret this, Serenity!" She screamed, her voice echoing down the halls. "You fucked with the wrong one!"

As Serenity was wheeled out, her bloodied hand clutching the stretcher's edge, she locked eyes with Cartier for a brief moment. In his gaze, she saw his fear and his love.

The courtroom had descended into chaos, but Serenity's fight wasn't over. It was just beginning. And now, with the world watching, the truth would be impossible to silence.

Chapter Sixteen

Aftermath

The courthouse doors swung open, unleashing a storm of flashing cameras and a deafening of shouting voices. Cartier Richardson stepped out, his jaw set like stone, his eyes steely as they faced the media frenzy. Beside him, Callie Morgan clung to his arm, her emerald eyes sharp and watchful, scanning the crowd with a mixture of caution and defiance.

"Mr. Richardson! How does it feel to be exonerated?" a reporter thrust a microphone towards Cartier's face.

Cartier's lips curled into a practiced smile, but his eyes remained cold. "Justice has prevailed," he declared, his rich baritone carrying over the clamor. "The truth always comes to light, no matter how deep the shadows."

Callie leaned in, her hair cascading over her shoulder as she whispered, "Careful, darling. Every word is a weapon now."

Cartier nodded; the relief of freedom warred with the simmering rage at the betrayal that had landed him here. He longed to lash out, to name names and expose the rot at the core of CR Enterprises. But strategy demanded patience.

"We're grateful for the support of our friends and colleagues," Callie interjected, her voice a melody of charm. "CR Enterprises remains committed to excellence and innovation."

As they navigated the gauntlet of reporters, Cartier's thoughts drifted to Serenity. Her testimony had been the key to his freedom, but at what cost?

Miles away, in a sterile hospital room, Serenity

stared at the ceiling, her body a canvas of pain and tubes. The muted TV in the corner showed Cartier and Callie's triumphant exit from the courthouse.

"You did it," she whispered to herself, a blend of pride and anguish coloring her words. "You saved him."

But at what cost? Lila's betrayal still burned; the phantom pain of the gunshot wound a constant reminder of how close she'd come to losing everything. Serenity closed her eyes, memories washing over her like a tide.

"I exposed you, Lila," she thought, her inner voice tinged with bitterness. "But you nearly took me with you."

Serenity's fingers ghosted over the bandages on her abdomen. The physical wound would heal, but the emotional scars ran deeper. She had played a dangerous game, dancing on the razor's edge between truth and deception.

"Was it worth it?" she asked the empty room. The silence offered no answers, only the steady beep of monitors and the weight of choices made.

As Cartier's face filled the TV screen once more, Serenity felt a familiar tug in her chest. Relief at his freedom warred with the lingering doubt about her own role in this intricate web of lies and loyalty.

"What comes next, Cartier?" she murmured, her eyes fixed on his image. "And where do I fit in your grand design now?"

The questions hung in the air, unanswered, as Serenity drifted into an uneasy sleep, the chess pieces of power and betrayal still moving on the board of her dreams.

The stark fluorescent light flickered, casting ominous shadows across Lila Richardson's face as she sat rigid in her jail cell. Her manicured nails dug crescents into her palms, rage simmering just beneath her carefully composed exterior.

"Serenity," she hissed, the name tasting like venom on her tongue. "You think you've won, don't you?"

Lila's mind raced, calculating, plotting. The cold metal of the cell bars beneath her fingertips fueled her fury.

"You've made a grave mistake, my dear," she uttered, a twisted smile playing at the corners of her mouth. "I controlled an empire. I can—and will—do it again."

The sound of footsteps echoing down the corridor snapped Lila from her lingering thoughts. She straightened, pressing her jumpsuit with an air of disdain.

"They think these walls can hold me?" she fumed, her eyes glinting with malice. "Oh, how little they know."

As the guard passed, Lila's thoughts turned to her vast network of connections—pawns waiting to be moved across the board.

"Enjoy your momentary triumph, Serenity," she whispered. "Because when I'm done, you'll wish you'd never crossed Lila Richardson."

Sunlight filtered softly through the hospital blinds, creating soft patterns on the walls of Serenity's room. The faint hum of machinery and the rhythmic beep of the heart monitor filled the otherwise quiet space. The door creaked open, and Audra and Donovan stepped inside, their expressions exuding concern and quiet admiration.

Audra was the first to speak, her voice warm but tinged with unease. "Serenity," she said delicately her eyes scanning the bandages and monitors, "how are you holding up?"

Serenity mustered a faint smile, her wit intact despite her weakened state. "Like I've been shot," she quipped, wincing slightly as she shifted in bed. "But, you know, I'm managing."

Audra sighed, a trace of relief crossing her face, while Donovan shook his head, his usual stoicism giving way to a rare flicker of amusement.

"Leave it to you to crack jokes after what just happened," he said, his voice gruff but affectionate. "You're something else, Serenity."

"Wouldn't be me if I didn't," she replied, her determination shining through the pain.

"We have news," Donovan announced, exchanging a glance with Audra. "All the evidence against Lila and Bradley has been handed over to the prosecutor."

Serenity's heart raced, her mind reeling with the implications. "And?" she prompted, her voice barely above a whisper.

Audra's lips curved into a satisfied smile. "It's damning, Serenity. You did it. You brought down Lila and exposed the corruption within CR Enterprises."

"You're amazing," Donovan added, his eyes conveying a depth of emotion rarely seen. "Your bravery in testifying, even at great personal risk... it's commendable."

Serenity closed her eyes, relief washing over her like a warm wave. But beneath the surface, doubt still lingered. "And what of the consequences?" she asked, her gaze flicking between Audra and Donovan. "The fallout for the company?"

Audra's expression tightened. "There will be challenges ahead," she admitted. "But thanks to you, we have a chance to rebuild CR Enterprises with integrity."

As Serenity processed their words, a trace of movement outside her room caught her attention. A familiar silhouette passed by, sending her heart into a frenzy.

Was that...? No, it couldn't be. Not yet.

Serenity turned back to Audra and Donovan once more, "I couldn't have done it without you both. We are a team, and all deserve credit for this."

The sleek private jet idled on the tarmac, its engines humming softly as Bradley Upton strode toward it, his tailored suit crisp and immaculate despite the long week behind him. The setting sun cast a warm glow over the airstrip, but Bradley's thoughts were far from serene. He clutched a leather briefcase tightly, his expression calm, though his mind churned with plans for damage control. He was always one step ahead—or so he thought.

Just as he reached the base of the stairs, the distant sound of sirens cut through the evening air. Bradley paused, his brow furrowing. He turned, his gaze sweeping the tarmac as a convoy of black SUVs screeched to a halt nearby. Doors flew open, and federal agents poured out, their badges glinting in the light.

"Bradley Upton!" one of them called out, his voice firm and authoritative. "This is the FBI. Step away from the aircraft and put your hands where we can see them."

Bradley's jaw tightened, but his mask of composure didn't falter. He raised his hands slowly, his briefcase slipping to the ground. "This is a mistake," he said with conviction, his voice calm but edged with irritation. "Whatever you think you have on me, I assure you, it's nothing."

The lead agent approached. "You're under arrest for conspiracy, fraud, racketeering, and multiple other charges tied to Lila Richardson and CR Enterprises." He gestured to his team, who swiftly closed in. "We have a warrant."

Bradley barely blinked as the cold steel of handcuffs clicked around his wrists. "You're making a very big mistake," he said evenly, his tone almost bored. "You'll see soon enough."

The agent didn't respond, instead nodding to his colleagues to escort Bradley toward one of the waiting vehicles. The briefcase remained abandoned on the tarmac, its contents of no concern now.

As Bradley was led away, the jet's engines powered down, its promise of escape extinguished. For the first time, the cracks in Bradley's carefully curated façade began to show. He glanced back at the jet, then at the agents surrounding him, his confidence waning as the reality of his situation sank in.

The lead agent leaned in slightly as they reached the SUV. "You've been one step ahead for a long time, Upton. But not anymore."

Without another word, Bradley was loaded into the vehicle, his once-unshakable world collapsing with every passing second.

The steady hum of machines and the sterile scent of disinfectant had become all too familiar to Serenity over the past few days. The sunlight streaming through the hospital blinds felt almost intrusive, casting harsh light on her bandaged side and the stark reality of her recovery. She had spent the last few days replaying the courtroom chaos in her mind, the sound of Lila's gunshot echoing like a haunting refrain.

The door to her hospital room creaked open, breaking the heavy silence. Serenity turned her head, expecting Audra or Donovan, but instead, she was met with Cartier Richardson's unmistakable silhouette. His imposing figure filled the doorway, a stark contrast to the vulnerability she felt lying in the hospital bed.

He was immaculately dressed in a tailored navy suit that accentuated his athletic frame, paired with a crisp white shirt and a silk tie that caught the sunlight just enough to glint. Every detail, down to the polished leather shoes, spoke of precision and power.

There was no sign that this man had only recently been behind bars. If anything, he looked more like he was stepping off the cover of a magazine than out of a jail cell.

"Cartier," she said softly, her voice carrying equal parts surprise and wariness.

As he approached, his movements deliberate but uncharacteristically hesitant, as though unsure of his welcome.

She shifted slightly in the bed, biting back a wince as the movement tugged at her wound.

"Serenity," he said, his voice warm but tinged with something she couldn't quite identify—gratitude, anger, or perhaps even guilt.

She studied him, gazing over his perfectly collected exterior. "You clean up well," she remarked jokingly, leaning back against the pillows. "No one would guess you just walked out of a courtroom circus—or a prison cell, for that matter."

His lips twitched into the faintest semblance of a smile, but his eyes remained serious. "I've learned that appearances are everything," he replied, slipping his hands into his pockets. "And you... you look beautiful as always, especially considering."

"Considering I was shot?" she said lightly, arching an eyebrow.

"Considering the war you've just declared,"

Cartier countered, his voice dropping slightly, concern consuming his face. "Lila is already dangerous—now she's desperate."

"I'm not afraid of Lila," Serenity said, meeting his stare head-on.

Cartier studied her for a moment, the intensity in her eyes unwavering. "Maybe you should be," he said quietly.

Serenity's smile was defiant. "Let her come," she said, her voice steady despite the bandages and the beeping monitors around her. "She's underestimated me for the last time."

Cartier leaned against the windowsill, crossing his arms as he watched her. "You're playing a dangerous game, Serenity. But then again... you've always been good at winning."

Her eyes gleamed with determination. "This isn't just a game, Cartier," she said softly. "This is the endgame."

Serenity met his eyes, her expression softening despite herself.

Cartier moved closer, pulling a chair to her bedside but not sitting. "Lila's gone off the rails. She's desperate, and that makes her dangerous. What you did in court..." He paused, the words hanging in the air like a challenge. "It's changed everything."

"That was the point," Serenity said simply, her voice rising.

Cartier leaned forward slightly, his elbows resting on his knees, his face now mere inches from hers. "You've declared war on her, Serenity. Are you ready for what comes next?"

"I've been ready for a long time."

"You risked everything - your life, your reputation - to expose the truth. To save me from my own blindness." His voice cracked with emotion. "I've never loved you more than I do right now."

Serenity's eyes widened as Cartier reached into his pocket, producing a familiar velvet box. Her engagement ring - the one she had reluctantly left at his penthouse - glinted in the harsh hospital lighting.

"Serenity Clayborn," Cartier said, his voice low and fervent, "will you still be my wife?"

"Of course!" Serenity beamed,

From a distance, Callie watched in shock as Cartier slid the engagement ring onto Serenity's finger. "You will never marry her," Callie snapped, her voice a poisonous whisper.

"Enjoying the show?" Donovan's measured voice startled her.

She turned to him, her emerald eyes blazing. "Cartier doesn't belong with her. He never did."

Donovan crossed his arms, his calm demeanor a stark contrast to her fury. "And you think he belongs with you? After everything that's happened?"

Callie remained defiant. "You think I'm going to just walk away? After all I've been through? After everything I gave up for him?"

She turned back to the window, watching as Cartier gently took Serenity's hand, his voice soft and too muffled for her to hear. The sight only hardened her resolve.

"Callie—" Donovan started, but she cut him off, her tone cold and final.

"This isn't over," she said, her glare never leaving Cartier. "Serenity won't win. I won't let her. Not after all the sacrifices I've made for him."

Donovan's advice hardened. "Let it go, Callie. Your freedom is a gift - don't squander it on this obsession. Cartier has made his choice."

Callie's nails dug deeper into her palms as Donovan's words landed, but she didn't flinch. Her eyes stayed locked on Cartier and Serenity inside the room, their silhouettes framed by the warm light spilling into the hallway. Serenity, fragile but defiant, and Cartier, looking at her with a tenderness Callie had never seen. It stung, cutting deeper than she'd thought possible.

"Serenity might have his attention now, but she will never have his heart."

As Callie turned and walked away, her heels echoed sharply against the cold, sterile floor, each step a declaration of her unyielding resolve. Donovan remained in the hallway, his gaze fixed on her retreating figure, a heavy mix of pity and dread clouding his expression. But Callie didn't care. In her mind, the outcome was already sealed. Serenity Clayborn might believe she had won, but Callie Morgan was playing the long game—and she never lost.

Coming Soon

Callie's Cartel

A KING PRODUCTION

Baller Bitches
VOLUME 1

A NOVEL

JOY DEJA KING

Diamond

"Bitch, you ain't shit!" When my baby daddy stood in front of me screaming that bullshit with spit flying everywhere, I kept putting the clear coat of polish on my nails ignoring his ass. "Did you hear what the fuck I said?" he belted as the vein in the middle of his forehead started pulsating.

"Mutherfucka, everybody in the damn building can hear what the fuck you just said. Are you done ranting 'cause I got shit to do?"

"That's what's wrong wit yo' ass, yo' mouth too fuckin' slick."

"Umm this shit gettin' repetitive. Ain't but so many ways you can call me a bitch and tell me I ain't shit. I get it, you think I'm foul. So either come up with some new descriptions or move on to something else."

"I can't believe I got a baby wit' yo' stupid ass. You don't give a fuck about nobody but yourself. One day I promise I'ma take our daughter away from you because I refuse to let her grow up and end up like you."

I put my polish down and eyeballed Rico because I wanted him to know what I was about to say wasn't a game. "Nigga, the day you start plotting to take my daughter away from me is the day you better tell yo' mama to start making your funeral arrangements. You can call me every ho, dick sucker, no good bitch all mutherfuckin' day but when you bring Destiny into the mix we have a problem. Now please get the fuck out my crib and take that noise you spewing someplace else."

"Diamond, this shit ain't over. I'll be back tomorrow to pick up my daughter for the weekend and she better be here and not at your mother's house."

"I tell you what. Why don't you pick Destiny up from my mother's house tomorrow because I can't take having to see yo' ass two days in a row."

"No, I'll pick Destiny up from here tomorrow. So whatever partying and fucking you planning on doing tonight make sure you have yo' ass up in time to get my daughter in the morning."

"That's what your problem is now. So busy worrying about what the fuck I'm doing," I huffed under my breath not wanting to reignite the argument because I was ready for Rico to bounce.

"Bye," I said keeping my head down, until I heard the door shut.

There was a time an argument with Rico would fuck up my entire day but this shit had become so routine I barely broke a sweat over it now. See, there was a time when Rico was actually my boyfriend. I thought we would be together forever but that was when I was young and dumb. He swooped me up when I was fifteen and not used to good dick or money. When I was walking home from school one afternoon he pulled up in a tricked out Benz and I couldn't believe when he rolled down the window asking me for my name. He was one of those pretty niggas who knew his packaging was right.

From that day on we started dating. Rico would pick me up from school almost everyday and them chick's mouths dropped every time he pulled up and I would get in the car. We would go get something to eat and just talked. Although he was three years older than me he never made me feel like a kid instead I felt like a woman. But I wasn't a woman and Rico was way out of my league. He quickly made me his girl but that didn't keep him from having mad other bitches, so many I couldn't keep count. In the beginning I fell for all his lies. He had a valid excuse for every accusation I had. By the time I woke up to the truth it was two years later and I was pregnant with Destiny.

That was the roughest nine months of my life.

I had bitches calling my phone harassing me. They would say my man just left their crib and he fucked the shit out of them. My feet swelled up, belly poked out feeling depressed and helpless having to hear this shit. By this time, Rico wasn't even trying to hide his dirt anymore. He felt I was pregnant and stuck. Even after all that I stayed with Rico. It took another year before I wised up and gave that nigga the deuces. When I did, Rico tried to make my life a living hell. I guess he thought I would be a dumbass forever...not!

I spent the first year of Destiny's life being with her day and night while Rico ran the streets. I don't even remember him changing one diaper. But I loved her so much it didn't even matter. Destiny was like my real life baby doll and she helped me get my shit together. I had gained so much weight during my pregnancy and even more afterwards and I think it was out of depression, because Rico had me so stressed out. I decided I had to get myself back on point and I started taking Destiny out in her stroller everyday. Within six months I had walked all that weight off. After that you couldn't tell me nothing, including Rico. I went from being a sad, miserable bitch to a baller bitch.

Coming Soon

Baller Bitches
Volume 5 — Full Circle

P.O. Box 912
Collierville, TN 38027

A KING PRODUCTION

www.joydejaking.com
www.twitter.com/joydejaking

ORDER FORM

| Name: |
| Address: |
| City/State: |
| Zip: |

QUANTITY	TITLES	PRICE	TOTAL
	Bitch	$17.99	
	Bitch Reloaded	$17.99	
	The Bitch Is Back	$17.99	
	Queen Bitch	$17.99	
	Last Bitch Standing	$17.99	
	Superstar	$17.99	
	Ride Wit' Me	$17.99	
	Ride Wit' Me Part 2	$17.99	
	Stackin' Paper	$17.99	
	Trife Life To Lavish	$17.99	
	Trife Life To Lavish II	$17.99	
	Stackin' Paper II	$17.99	
	Rich or Famous	$17.99	
	Rich or Famous Part 2	$17.99	
	Rich or Famous Part 3	$17.99	
	Bitch A New Beginning	$17.99	
	Mafia Princess Part 1	$17.99	
	Mafia Princess Part 2	$17.99	
	Mafia Princess Part 3	$17.99	
	Mafia Princess Part 4	$17.99	
	Mafia Princess Part 5	$17.99	
	Boss Bitch	$17.99	
	Baller Bitches Vol. 1	$17.99	
	Baller Bitches Vol. 2	$17.99	
	Baller Bitches Vol. 3	$17.99	
	Bad Bitch	$17.99	
	Still The Baddest Bitch	$17.99	
	Power	$17.99	
	Power Part 2	$17.99	
	Drake	$17.99	
	Drake Part 2	$17.99	
	Female Hustler	$17.99	
	Female Hustler Part 2	$17.99	

QUANTITY	TITLES	PRICE	TOTAL
	Female Hustler Part 3	$17.99	
	Female Hustler Part 4	$17.99	
	Female Hustler Part 5	$17.99	
	Female Hustler Part 6	$17.99	
	Princess Fever "Birthday Bash"	$6.00	
	Nico Carter The Men Of The Bitch Series	$17.99	
	Bitch The Beginning Of The End	$17.99	
	Supreme...Men Of The Bitch Series	$17.99	
	Bitch The Final Chapter	$17.99	
	Stackin' Paper III	$17.99	
	Men Of The Bitch Series And The Women Who Love Them	$17.99	
	Coke Like The 80s	$17.99	
	Baller Bitches The Reunion Vol. 4	$17.99	
	Stackin' Paper IV	$17.99	
	The Legacy	$17.99	
	Lovin' Thy Enemy	$17.99	
	Stackin' Paper V	$17.99	
	The Legacy Part 2	$17.99	
	Assassins - Episode 1	$12.99	
	Assassins - Episode 2	$12.99	
	Assassins - Episode 3	$12.99	
	Bitch Chronicles	$40.00	
	So Hood So Rich	$17.99	
	Stackin' Paper VI	$17.99	
	Female Hustler Part 7	$17.99	
	Toxic...	$12.99	
	Stackin' Paper VII	$17.99	
	Sugar Babies...	$12.99	
	Deadly Divorce...	$12.99	
	The Legacy Part 3	$17.99	
	BITCH The Story of Precious Cummings	$17.99	
	Mastermind...	$12.99	
	Stackin' Paper VIII	$17.99	
	Stackin' Paper Holiday	$12.99	
	Mastermind 2...	$12.99	

Shipping/Handling (Via Priority Mail) $9.85 1-3 Books, $18.40 4-10 Books. For 11 or more $24.75. Total: $_____ FORMS OF ACCEPTED PAYMENTS: Certified or government issued checks and money Orders, all mail in orders take 5-7 Business days to be delivered

www.ingramcontent.com/pod-product-compliance
Lightning Source LLC
Chambersburg PA
CBHW022036220526
45357CB00059B/275